the **americas**

The Fish Child

The Fish Child

Lucía Puenzo

Translated by David William Foster

Texas Tech University Press

Work published within the framework of "Sur" Translation Support Program of the Ministry of Foreign Affairs, International Trade and Worship of the Argentine Republic.

   The publisher and author appreciate the financial support for translation of *The Fish Child*.

This book is typeset in Fairfield. The paper used in this book meets the minimum requirements of ANSI/NISO Z39.48-1992 (R1997). ∞

Designed by Barbara Werden

Library of Congress Cataloging-in-Publication Data
Puenzo, Lucía.
   [Niño pez. English]
   The fish child / Lucía Puenzo ; translated by David William Foster.
      p. cm. — (The Americas)
      Summary: "The sordid, thrilling, and comic story of two young lovers—affluent Lala and impoverished Guayi; examines the economic and social circumstances of Argentina and Paraguay to make sense of the characters' past choices and present misfortunes. Translated by David William Foster"—Provided by publisher.
      ISBN 978-0-89672-714-4 (hardcover : alk. paper)
      1. Satire. 2. Paraguay—Fiction. 3. Argentina—Fiction. I. Foster, David William. II. Title.
   PQ7798.426.U36N5613 2010
   863'.7—dc22   2010024465

Printed in the United States of America
10 11 12 13 14 15 16 17 18 / 9 8 7 6 5 4 3 2 1

Texas Tech University Press | Box 41037 | Lubbock, Texas 79409-1037 USA
800.832.4042 | ttup@ttu.edu | www.ttupress.org

For Sergio Bizzio

What powerful force is this that drives a coward
to kill an innocent person?

R. AKUTAGAWA

The Fish Child

It could have been worse, believe me. It took them a day to make up their minds. Prodan. Saumerio. Violeta. I imagined myself going out into the world like Violeta and I peed my pants hiding in corners. Let's see if you get me: I'm black, macho, and bad. No matter how I look right now, with tubes coming out of me, on the verge of being dead meat. It was an accident, something that could happen to anyone. And what they're saying is not true: I'm not stupid, just curious. If I see something moving beneath the leaves . . . I bite. Sorry, I digress, I know . . . it isn't easy when Lala caresses me this way. And it doesn't look good, a dying dog with an erection.

But what excites me, more than her caresses, are her tears. Because Lala never cries. She didn't cry when Guayi left her or when Brontë died. Her chin trembled a bit the day she saw me in the cage. She had eyes for no one else. Although the bitch of a veterinarian told her that the one next to me had a better snout, she wanted me. She didn't stop talking to me until we got home (she always treated me like an adult). And that day we sealed our pact: I was a present for Sasha, her mother, but I belong to her. I peed on her a bit, so she'd know I understood. And she did.

When we got home, Sasha grabbed me from Lala's arms.

"Saumerio!" she cried.

I made a panoramic sweep of my new home from the air. I opened my mouth and barked for the first time, which was ridiculous I know, but life began to be good. The first thing I saw was the Paraguayan girl, an adolescent maid. Guayi, as I call her between us, is stronger than any of the other protagonists of the adult films Lala and I would watch until dawn. She was doing a cleansing with a stick of incense.

"Say hello to him!" Sasha cried out.

Guayi smiled with her white teeth with no decays. Pep raised his head up from the arm chair.

"If you call him Saumerio he's going to turn out a little fairy dog. Call him Prodan."

And he disappeared behind a copy of the *Diary of Che*. Pep, with his tiny name, wants to change the world. His friends call him that because it's hard for him to get through the day without a hit of LSD.* The last one I saw was Brontë. He lowered his newspaper, took a toothpick out of his mouth, and said, "Name him Violeta and teach him to jump."

The fat man's weird. I don't have to give any explanations after a statement like that. He's important, publishes books, and people come by to interview him. But when he's among family all he does is say dumb jokes. Even if out in the world they think he's a genius, he has no talent. Even when he throws me a stick, he's the one who most has something up his sleeve.

"Show him a piece of bread and you'll see how he jumps. That's all they know how to do," Brontë said, looking down Guayi's dress.

---

* A dose of LSD is called Pepa in Argentina.

Lala looked at the fat man with disgust. She couldn't understand him. More than one night I found her reading his books. She would underline them, write summaries, memorize questions. She would park herself in front of the closed door of his study to listen to his interviews. Only once did she get up the courage to knock. I followed her in and bared my teeth at the fat man.

"What do you want?" he asked.

Lala told him she didn't understand the thesis of his last book. Did he really believe there was no hope for our country? Brontë lifted his fingers from the keyboard.

"You don't understand a thing I write. They're all lies."

He put his cigarette out on the desk and went on writing.

Lala spent the night face down on her bed, biting her pillow. She tried to smother herself. I did what I could: I licked her feet. I did it for hours, so she wouldn't feel so alone. When she fell asleep, I tore the pages out of the fat man's book. I left the scraps, slobbered all over, at the door of the study. Lala awoke at dawn and didn't scold me when she saw me swallowing the last pages. She went into the bathroom and lifted the top of the toilet so she could flush them down the drain. But that was quite a bit later.

The day of the panoramic sweep, Sasha drew me to her face and rubbed my nose with hers. Every time I think of her I remember her that way, deformed and cross-eyed, asking me, "And what sort of name would you like?"

"Vomit," I thought before opening my mouth.

So, as you will see, I didn't get off to a good start with Sasha either. I dropped to the floor; she went off to wipe her silk robe and didn't touch me again until evening.

"Serafín," she told them when they were all together again for dinner.

Everyone nodded, watching the television set. Guayi was the only one to pat me on the head.

"Otorere ombogue," she said.

And she continued to serve the mashed potatoes. She liked to say things no one understood like, "it could have been worse." I can still close my eyes and see our first family meal together. No one looked at anyone else and no one said anything to anyone else. The only two who looked at each other were Guayi and Lala. They brushed against each other and were always touching each other. If you only knew the things that went on in there. As far as the world was concerned, the Brontës were just one more family in San Isidro. Lala and Pep went to a private college, one that was Scottish. They came home at five o'clock and locked themselves in their bedrooms until dinner time. Sasha had left economics for esoteric matters. She wore tunics, cured trees by sprinkling them with Bach's Flowers, and was convinced I liked Animal Planet. The fat man only left his study for the interviews. Those were the only nights the Brontës, when they looked at the camera, seemed to look at us and talk to us.

On Sundays he would take me out for a walk on the bike path. I did the social bit, hoping to run into frigid bitches, but ones from good families, and he would give me a kick in the butt every time I wandered away from him. When we returned, he always said the same thing to Sasha: "A little stroll with me and he's like new." Then he'd rub my butt and lock himself in to work.

And, yes, the day was shitty. That's why I spent it sleeping, to prepare myself. Because nighttime in the Brontë house was a party. At midnight Pep would put me in the car with him. He would brake at the corner of the fanciest dive in San Isidro and would spend the night driving around, always with a client on board, selling marihuana. He would say the same thing to everyone, that it was Super Skunk, imported directly from Holland . . . that he had planted it in the garden he kept on the roof of his house. And it was true, except that Pep and his friends smoked the weed he grew in his garden. What he sold he bought in Los Chinos, the slum behind the Coastal Train.

He would take me there, too. And everything he got there he would try out first with me. He injected me with heroin, rubbed cocaine on my gums, made me try the Special K just in case the pellets were old. He would say that these days it was better to be sure of what you had because they would sell you anything. And he wasn't wrong about that: one night a line of coke left me stiff as a board. I couldn't even bark.

Let's go back now to Guayi. At exactly two o'clock, Guayi would cross the house in shadows and open the door for Guida, the security guard. I would wait for them in the bedroom, under the bed. And I would not come out until Guida closed the door and put out the light.

"Eche ruve cheve larey potava. Coete dia otoca ndeve . . . ," Guayi would say as she took his clothes off.

"Always otoca cheve. Otoca ndeve," Guida would reply.

How I miss that darkness filled with whispering in Guaraní! She always asked him for the same thing, which was to call her Miss Lala . . . and she made him say it over and over again. She seemed the stronger of the two, Guayi, but she was the only one to cry. She would cry when she heard Sasha and Brontë yelling at each other. When Pep would grab her ass in front of his friends. When Lala would not open the door even when she begged. Sometimes she would cry in the middle of a sentence, for no reason at all; and often other times in front of the fishbowl that Lala had in her bedroom. It was the only thing they argued about: Guayi would get mad whenever Lala would bring a new fish home in a plastic bag and even more so when she would discover her staring at her fish as though hypnotized. She asked her why she had them.

"To watch them."

And that was when the yelling would begin. As far as Guayi was concerned that wasn't a good reason to have them buried that way. She didn't understand that it wasn't their tomb, but rather their home. She would talk in her sleep in Guaraní. Some nights she would let me come in and we would sleep in each other's arms, with the moon framed in the window. "Ochaju chasy," Guayi would call them (moon baths).

The last night she saw Guida was Lala's birthday. Just like every year, Lala didn't want a party (she had no friends). She blew the candles out and shut herself up in her room with a piece of cake. She waited until the house was quiet before going downstairs to look for Guayi. She was going to tell her that she loved her. And she didn't care if everyone knew it. But before knocking on the door, she heard Guayi's moans mixed with Guida's voice. He kept repeating the same thing: "Miss Lala." I smelled her on the other side of the door. And I barked until Guayi got up from the bed and opened the door . . . and froze when she saw Lala in the shadows.

"Tell him to get out," Lala told her, "tell him to get out right now."

Guayi went back in the room and reappeared a minute later with Guida, each one wearing their uniform. Guida began to say Miss, but Lala stuck in his throat and he walked on by without looking at her.

"Do you love him?" Lala asked her when Guayi sat down next to her.

"No . . ."

"Don't see him again. Not him and not anyone else," Lala said, and raised her arm to caress her. But something made her stop scared in mid-air and her arm suddenly dropped and she caressed me.

"I want you to be my girlfriend."

"Tell me in Guaraní."

"I don't know how you say it . . ."

"Roaychy. Roypota che chycara."

"Ro ai chi . . ."

"No. Ro jai ju . . . roy potá ye yicara . . . ," Guayi said, and it sounded like she was singing.

Lala had to say it a couple of times before Guayi, laughing, covered her mouth with a kiss. They stayed there, kissing each other on the kitchen floor, until dawn. Guayi never opened the door again for Guida. She couldn't have: He died a few weeks later trying to stop some kids who were holding up an old man. People said that one of the kids shot him in the stomach. And that Guida got him before he checked out. I know the kid he killed. I had seen him with Lala a couple of weeks before, down by the river. If there is anything I never forget it's the people who throw me a stick to fetch. And the kid did it for about an hour while he talked to Lala. Before we left, she gave him a pair of little chains that belonged to Sasha and he gave me the stick.

But who cares about Guida. What matters is that something happened to them after that night. But it was no use. Something was up and we were all wondering what it was. It was the same with Brontë: before, he would jack off with the photograph of his wife. His imagination was not even big enough for that. Now, from the window of his study, he watched how Guayi washed down the patio, how she waxed the floors . . . and how she would lie down on the freshly cut lawn with her hair undone to catch a half hour of sun before Lala got home from school. I spent my time on the living room cushions. I bit them; I fucked them in twos and threes. . . .

On the days Sasha was not at home, Lala would strip off her uniform at the door and jump in the pool. I would run around the edges, wagging my tail and barking. Guayi would wait for her on the stairs holding a towel. Then they would have a glass of milk together, while Lala showed her what she had learned that day. Guayi pretended to understand, but she wasn't interested. All she wanted was for Lala to learn to speak Guaraní. They dreamed about going to Paraguay and living together. Not in the capital, but in Ypacaraí.

In the morning while they were taking a bath together, Lala leaned her back against Guayi's tits and listened to her talk about the blue lake in Ypacaraí. About how she would swim for hours around her grandfather's canoe, looking at the rich people's houses while the old man fished. They would linger in the water making plans, until their skin was wrinkled. They were going to buy a plot of land on the banks of the river. And Guayi was going to design their dream house. Before going to bed they would count their savings, which they kept in a mayonnaise jar. Any loose bill they found in Brontë's pockets or in Sasha's purse would end up in the jar.

Sasha hadn't been able to stand the Paraguayan for quite some time, but Brontë forbade her from hiring anyone else. Sasha was never very insistent, because her head was also full of plans: in a week she would be on her way to another congress on Flores de Bach, in Pennsylvania (in reality, she was off to India with her lover).

Guayi no longer took her days off. She would stay at home on Sundays, but dressed in Lala's clothes. They were inseparable in recent months. Lala missed school more and more and Guayi cleaned the house less and less. They had even begun to look alike, in black and white.

"This isn't normal. . . . We've got to do something . . . ," Sasha said to Brontë as she watched them play with a water hose in the garden, both of them soaked in their tiny bikinis.

She had found him watching them from his study window and had mistaken his heavy breathing for concern.

"For once she's got a friend. Leave her alone," Brontë said, zipping up his pants.

"No way . . . She can't be friends with the maid. . . ."

Lala looked up and smiled when she saw them. Now that she was in love she liked them.

"Serafín, come and get a bath," she yelled at me.

I ran off, stumbled, and rolled down the stairs. I reached the door the moment Guayi opened it to look for me. I pretended to run away (they would have found it suspicious if I gave in to the bath without a struggle), but I could already feel my whole self coming alive as I thought of their hands rubbing me all over. I let them drag me off, digging my nails into the lawn. Guayi put my tail between her legs and Lala my head between hers.

"What will we do with him when we leave?" Guayi asked.

"Take him with us," Lala said without doubting for a second.

I cried.

And not because of the soap that had gotten into my eyes. I cried baring my teeth and shaking by behind (emotion does that to me).

"Poor little thing. He's hot," Lala said tenderly.

Poor little thing?

The bitch next door is in heat.

Without another word, they ran in to get dressed and fetch my leash. Fifteen minutes later Guayi opened the front door to the house next door. Lala called to Cleo with a piece of meat. They led us to a plaza and tied the bitch to a tree.

"She's all yours," Lala said.

The bitch was a royal mess. I showed her my teeth so she would understand that I wouldn't be able to do anything with them looking on. And Lala, as always, understood. She grabbed Guayi and they disappeared around to the other side of the giant ombú.

I did what I had to do. But it was tough, because Cleo was about as exciting as a pillow. On the way back home she held her head down and was depressed (her twat hurt, as she was no longer a virgin and could tell when she looked at me that her pups would end up ugly as sin). Lala and Guayi walked in front of us, holding hands. They could have walked through walls, hanging onto each other like that. I nipped Cleo so she would understand that things were fine between us. It wasn't her fault. There wasn't a bitch in the world that could hold a candle to the two of them.

Lala found out that afternoon. We were watching the last adult film we had gotten a hold of when Guayi knocked on the door. She was holding Pep's video camera in one hand and a bag of garbage in the other.

"Would you like me to dance for you?" she asked.

Without waiting for an answer she closed the door, gave the camera to Lala, and opened the shutters to the moon. Then she began to undress and to sing in Guaraní. Lala had to lean against the wall because she was trembling. And I knew then it was Guayi who was controlling the lot of us. The Brontës and the world.

Lala filmed it all without breathing. When she was done, Guayi grabbed the pile of videos and looked at Lala, asking for permission. If there's something I can't forget it's her eyes looking at Guayi go out of the room naked, with her uniform in one hand and the bag of garbage, full, in the other. I confess the scene moved me, but love is one thing and adult films are something else. I followed Guayi dragging the bag of garbage until she disposed of it, and then I had to knock the can over to salvage the videos. I was caught up in that, licking the leftover food from my favorite video, when I hear a stifled cry. I knew it before I saw it, because I would recognize his smell even at the bottom of the blue lake of Ypacaraí. With one hand he covered his mouth and with the other he held onto her by her head. Brontë's blue and white pajamas began to slip down with each thrust until they reached his slippers. When he was done he wiped his forehead with a handkerchief embroidered with Sasha's initials telling her to wake up at 8 o'clock a.m., because they were coming to interview him from Channel A.

I could have stayed behind to console Guayi, but Pep put the leash on me and dragged me to the door. That evening he sold marihuana to a detective wearing street clothes. The jerk didn't even catch on, although I was barking at him during the entire transaction (he was wearing loafers without socks). They came for him the next day, ransacked the place, and found the garden on the roof. Brontë became big news and within a week his books were bestsellers. Sasha moved her trip up and called Brontë from the airport in Mumbai to tell him she wasn't in Pennsylvania but on her way to a Buddhist temple. And that's how we ended up on our own.

The house was never the same again. In the first place, it was dirty. Guayi no longer did any cleaning. She didn't take the garbage out. She didn't do the shopping. She knew she was wanted for something else. And it was as if Brontë could sense that he had little time left. He sank into another one of his depressions when Sasha left. That's how Lala remembered her father: hibernating in his bed or locked up in his study, and it was forbidden in either case to bother him. We were all prepared for another failed attempt at suicide. Brontë had been perfecting his method since he was an adolescent, without success. Every one of his family members, including his children, had found him unconscious at least once. It was always pills, and he was always rescued.

When winter came, the yard was filled with undergrowth, and the pool was stagnant. Brontë was getting worse. In earlier depressions, the only time when he seemed to find life worth living was when he wrote (although then, more than at any other time, it was related to death: nothing excited him more than to imagine his readers searching for clues, enigmas, and answers in each one of his texts). Now he was not even attempting to write. He waited for his daughter to go to school and then shut himself up with Guayi in his study. Who knows why she never said anything. Perhaps because what they had saved so far was not enough. Lala begged for them to leave with what they had. But Guayi always answered the same: "No, not yet."

She said nothing more. But you could see it in her eyes: she wanted her house, two floors, yard, and pool. Lala began to sell off Sasha's clothes and her jewels. . . . And when she realized that Brontë didn't care, she followed up with the furniture. In two weeks they replaced the mayonnaise jar with a shoe box. They counted the money when it wouldn't close.

"Okay, now. Let's go," Guayi said.

Lala asked for a few more days because she had a buyer for the paintings. A dog trainer who was her only friend. More than buying them, he placed them, keeping for himself the twenty percent. It made no difference to Brontë, ten paintings more, ten paintings less. Guayi didn't have the courage to say that she couldn't stand it that Brontë spent more time in bed with her than anywhere else. She didn't have to. Although she tried not to believe it, Lala had suspected it for some time. Guayi's smell had changed.

Lala came home early the next day. The house was all quiet. I greeted her at the door, and for the first time in my life, I followed her up the stairs. She opened and closed her hands, digging her nails in her palms. I clamped up my butt (fear does that to me). She pushed the door of Brontë's room open. . . .

"You're home early," Guayi said without turning around to look at her.

She was on all fours, cleaning the rug. Lala did not respond. She turned around and saw Brontë reading at his desk. She sat down on the bed and rested her hand on the sheet, looking from one to the other. Brontë never read and the door to his study was never open. Then she felt her hand. Better, what her hand was touching. The bed was warm. Damp. She walked over to Guayi and placed that same hand between her legs. Guayi closed her eyes, not moving.

Lala shut herself in Pep's room, Guayi in hers, and Brontë in his study. I didn't eat that night. The telephone rang for hours but no one answered. Lala yanked the cord out before chopping up ten Super Skunk tablets. Then she poured two glasses of milk. She put sugar in one, and in the other, one spoonful of sugar and one spoonful of Super Skunk. One spoonful of sugar, one spoonful of Super Skunk. One spoonful of sugar, one spoonful of Super Skunk.

Brontë was disappointed to see that it was his daughter who brought him the glass of milk. Lala set the two glasses down on the desk and let her father choose one.

"We did this every night when I was a little girl, do you remember?"

"Mmm . . . ," Brontë answered, downing the milk in one gulp.

Lala cooled her feelings with a glass of milk. Even if it was only one time in his life, Brontë had attempted to lie to her not to hurt her feelings. It was the perfect ending. She kissed him on the forehead and softly closed the door to the study. She lay down not sure if she was going to wake up again. I licked her and nipped her until she kicked me out of the room. I couldn't let her fall asleep. I tried to knock the door down, I barked, I even growled for her to open up. I ran up and down the stairs (I don't know why). And one time when I was running up the stairs, I saw Brontë's legs stretched out behind the door. Then I stopped running. Lala tripped over me when she came out of her room. It was early morning. And I was so happy that instead of barking I said:

"Lala!"

But she didn't hear me, because she was opening the door of the study. I followed her, tramping on her shadow. She was afraid and not for the fat man. She didn't even touch Brontë. Nor did she read the note that Guayi had left her ("Oteve en Ypacarí," it said). Nor did she touch the shoe box (empty). Nor did she cry. I told her so, right?

She slept until noon the next day. She did ten laps in the pool. And we walked out without locking the door. The only thing she took was my cage. We left Brontë's Mercedes at the door of the terminal and placed the keys next to an old man who was sleeping under some boxes.

"We'll see each other in Paraguay," she said to me after buying the tickets, rubbing some drops on my gums.

And suddenly the world collapsed.

When I opened my eyes I was inside my cage and I'd peed myself. My only traveling companion was a Paraguayan Pekinese who was missing a leg. He told me to call him Maradona, although his real name is Tereré. He spent the whole trip telling me about the bitches in Ypacaraí. No purebreds, just mixes, neat gals, always up for a roll in the hay. I listened to him barking and all I could think about was swimming in the lake with Guayi and Lala. They could roll the credits over that image, with a good sound track. Something in Guaraní, sugary but hip.

Lala bought a couple of newspapers in Asunción and spent the afternoon reading them. She found what she was looking for in a box at the foot of the page: J. J. BRONTË FOUND MURDERED the headline said.

"Ypacaraí!" the driver yelled from the window of the bus.

On to Ypacaraí, among chickens and smells. I made the trip with half my body sticking out the window, and the world looked like it would never end. Lala spent her time staring at a photograph of Guayi submerged in the bathtub with her eyes and her mouth open in a silent scream. She kept turning it over, looking at her and then at the address that was written on the back of the photo.

I'm not going to lie to you: Ypacaraí may be the prettiest place in Paraguay, but from the outset it looked crappy to me. I missed my yard, my overstuffed chair, my plastic bone, because I was always an outcast but made myself into a bad-ass dude. Finally at the end of the day, limping, covered in dirt and bites, I began to blend in. But I had to put up a big fight to keep them from jumping my neck and smelling my ass.

We reached Guayi's house at dusk. And Lala, instead of ringing the bell, sat down to wait. If Guayi was home she'd come out sooner or later. And she preferred not to know if she wasn't at home. She spent the day watching the door. But when it started to rain the only one who came out was Charo, a poor old man who took five minutes to cross the dirt road with his two canes and five more to catch his breath.

"Mdaeico?" he asked, looking at Lala.

"I'm looking for your granddaughter."

And she showed him the photograph she was carrying.

3

That night Lala slept in the room where Guayi grew up until the age of fifteen when she went to work in Buenos Aires. Taped to the headboard of the bed was the only photograph that Charo had of his granddaughter: Guayi naked the day she learned to walk, standing at the edge of the lake. An American tourist had taken the photograph and, in an act of charity, had sent it to him by mail from Texas.

I slept outside, as those were the rules of the house. In reality they were the rules of the town. As it grew darker, the dirt streets became populated with animals. Dogs, cats, chickens. Some were alone, others in groups of two or three, without owners and without leashes, sniffing in corners as if everything belonged to everyone. Even the cats were frightening. After my crying for two hours, the old man threw me a blanket. I was busy with the blanket flying through the air and me on my hind legs trying to catch it when I saw Tereré. The image was so pathetic that I looked the other way to save us both from feeling ashamed. Too late, as he had already seen me knocked over by a moth-eaten blanket and I had seen him jumping around fucking the air behind two coupled dogs.

"Come on, Serafín. Let's not do that together," he said and turned to face me.

When the lake came into view at the end of a curve, Tereré ran to the edge, gave a leap with his three legs and dove in like a bomb.

"Come on, don't be a wimp. . . . What are you waiting for?"

I was waiting for everything. I had just seen her swimming toward me. Once on land she shook herself wiggling her hips. She opened her eyes and I thought I'd die.

"Ofidia . . . ," Tereré said, already running before even saying let's get out of here.

Until I felt her teeth in my neck, I had no idea that an angel could hurt me. I was wrong. She bit me so hard that the next day, when I limped home to Charo's house, I was suffering from anemia. Ofidia was a myth in Ypacaraí. A snake had bit her and she hadn't died. There was a rumor among the dogs that she was immortal, the property of the most popular actor in Paraguay. She lived in his summer home and her hobby was to destroy the dogs that invaded her territory. Lala was pushing a supermarket cart when she saw me. She had bought a TV and a video player with the last of her money. She hid me in her room and we spent the night watching the video of Guayi over and over again while she bandaged my wounds. At one point the old man came into the room and stood in a corner (Charo never slept, made no noise, and had no smell about him).

"Eipota anive rejaharo haengu doumo aveima. Oyetota chupeteta Ochoa chuhuate."

Lala turned the TV off, turned the light on, and told Charo that she hadn't understood a word.

"Put the dog outside," the old man repeated.

But that's not what he said. What he said was for her to stop

waiting for her. Guayi had been arrested at the border. She didn't
need to understand him. Lala knew that it would be a while
before Guayi showed up. What didn't get delayed was the ship-
ment. Shut up in her room, Lala opened the cassette holders of
the adult films Guayi had thrown into the garbage. Inside, in the
place of the videos, was the money that they had saved up
together, spread out over the bed. She put it back in the cassette
holders and didn't touch it again. She didn't show it to anyone,
not even the old man. Nor did she go down to the lake. She
spent her nights staring off into the distance from the roof of the
house and her days sitting on one of the benches in the station
awaiting the arrival of the buses.

And then, thanks to Ofidia, I bit the head of the snake and
Lala returned to life. I'm thankful to Ofidia because another one
of her hobbies is chopping up snakes. There's nothing she likes
more in life than parading herself before the dogs who spy on her
(we were always there, hidden in the brush, admiring her) with a
pair of smothered snakes in her mouth. Yesterday, in a burst of
love (toward Ofidia), I emerged from the brush and bit the head
of a snake that was fleeing from her.

"Mvaerotopa jeurere . . . ," Ofidia said, because she doesn't
speak a word of Spanish.

Tereré dragged me home to Charo's. He couldn't stop crying
and cussing at me. By the time I got there I was already having
convulsions and pulmonary edema. The last thing I saw was
Charo dressed as a woman. And the first thing I saw when I
came to on the gurney was the veterinarian coming out of the
bathroom dressed in a tuxedo. I guessed death was like that: no
tunnels, but a flash of madness before the blackout. But no, the

old man likes to relive his youth. And the veterinarian works at night as a croupier. He checked the serum before leaving for the casino and told Lala to make her goodbyes. There was no hope for my survival.

"You're not going anywhere, do you hear me?" Lala said when we were alone, holding my head up so I could look at her.

She started to tell me what we were going to do if I lived. The veterinarian called every hour. He always asked the same thing: "Has he died yet?"

And Lala would answer the same way: "No. He's still here."

At five in the morning, when Lala told him that I was still breathing, he ran over from the casino with a couple of gamblers who didn't believe him. When they saw me they began to place bets. In reality all of them bet I wouldn't live until the following morning and Lala doggedly bet the money she and Guayi had saved up that I was going to live. I must confess that I was ready to hang it up when I heard what she said. Better, how she said it. She was her old self, just like she was when she had once kicked Pep in the jaw for shutting me in the closet with an overdose.

"She believes in me."

I repeated it all night long: "She believes in me!"

At seven in the morning the door to the veterinarian's was crowded with neighbors and dogs. And I began to feel the air in my lungs. I say that Lala came to life because I could feel that the woman pushing me in her supermarket cart was not the same woman who shut herself up for months in Guayi's room. She was swaying her hips in a gesture of triumph. And Tereré in front showing her the way to the lake.

"It's not that big or that blue. But it's not bad," Lala finally said.

Now she's seated at the edge of the lake, watching the dawn. She's just put her feet in the water. Ofidia is lying quietly at my side. Tereré is shooing off some dogs who are spying on me from the brush.

4

She decided to make use of the anxiety that was gnawing at her to begin on the house that she and Guayi had dreamed of, with the large picture windows facing the lake. The old man did not ask where the money had come from. He helped her choose a plot, three laborers, and a foreman with airs of an architect who became enthusiastic about the design. There was hunger and lack of employment in the town. In five days, when they laid down the foundation, we had already begun to forget what we had left behind. I had gotten used to sleeping on dirt and there was nothing more comforting for Lala than to fall into a deep sleep enveloped in Guayi's smell. She was the only one still with us and we could smell her in every corner of the room, with her fragrance of sweaty syrup. Her odor allowed us to see her dancing and we could hear her laughing. Just passing through her room was enough to keep her alive, in contrast to everything else, which began to lose shape and then overnight vanished from our memory.

The first thing that disappeared was the house, as there was no room for the domesticated smells of Acassuso, so intoxicated were we with Ypacaraí. Each space swallowed up its owner. Pep disappeared with his garden. Sasha with her bath oils, covered in creams. And Brontë with his office stinking of cigars. We didn't even miss them, and they ceased to exist.

Lala still ran down to await the arrival of each bus. But there was no sign of Guayi. One day she wouldn't move from the station until Charo convinced her to accompany him to the lake to fish. In the middle of the lake, Lala turned the oars over to the old man and jumped head-first into the water. She would come to do this often. She liked to swim until she was exhausted, her eyes and her mouth open, filling her body with water, always a little further down in the water. She tied a rope to the canoe and when she grew tired of swimming, she had the old man tow her.

One day she felt a small hand grab her foot. She tried to shake free but she couldn't. She turned around and saw a child about five years old down under the water smiling at her with his eyes open. His skin was so fine she could see his veins, his gray eyes, and protruding eyelashes, his green hair thick like algae. When Charo stopped rowing, the little boy let go of Lala's foot and swam between her legs with an impressive speed. He swam with his hands open and Lala was able to see that he had membranes between his fingers. Without a moment's hesitation she let go of the rope and swam after him until she was out of breath. I swam after the two of them nipping at their toes. I must have lost consciousness, because when I opened my eyes we were back in the boat, vomiting algae.

"Did you see him?" Lala asked the old man as soon as she could feel air in her lungs.

She tried to explain what she had seen. But it was no use, as there were days in which Charo did not understand Spanish.

"You did see him," she said to me.

She spent the evening drawing him on the cement walls. Every so often she would stop, look at me and repeat: "You saw him."

She said it to calm herself down, because she thought she was going mad. Her drawing had Guayi's face. She erased it with a wet cloth she rubbed over the carbon. Everything bothered her, even my breathing, even her clothes. She had forgotten the face she saw beneath the surface. She ended up naked, with the wind knotting her hair, making it dance like Ofidia's snakes. The sky crushed down on me. The house still had no roof and so the sky was inside the house. I lay down on my back, with my legs sticking up, supporting it. Then the moon came out. Lala's skin, the white walls . . . everything was tinted in blue. It was not the Buenos Aires moon, not even the moon at Charo's house. Suddenly, it was neither day nor night.

"Do you remember?" Lala said. Ochaju chasy . . .

She walked down to the dock and undid her robe. Don't imagine anything great. Just imagine a pair of rickety trunks tied together by an old rope. She lay down on her face and began to row. She only stopped when the skiff became suspended between the moon in the sky and the moon in the lake. Then she turned over, opened her arms and legs and lay still, as though nothing nor no one could harm her. She wanted to hold the moon within her. Now, then, imagine . . . imagine harder . . . so much so that you have to avert your gaze to keep on breathing. I felt on the back of my neck that the same thing was happening to someone else. I managed to see the outline of a man on the lot next door. I heard a moan and thought he was crying. But no. He was singing . . .

One warm night we met
next to the blue Lake Ypacaraí.
As you walked you sang in a sad voice
old melodies in Guaraní . . .

Ofidia was standing next to him, stoic about how his voice broke. She told me the next day that it was a song by Julio Iglesias. In reality it was an Indian song, until Julio Iglesias made it number one in the rankings and the whole world forgot about the Indians.

Where are you now, cuñataí?
I no longer hear your soft voice.
Where are you now?
I am frantic
and miss you body and soulllll . . .

Ofidia wrinkled up her nose until the man shut his mouth. Afterward, she trotted after him along the dirt road until they disappeared in the dark. It never crossed my mind that he could be her owner. One of the things I like about Ofidia is her fickleness. She's capable of taking a chunk out of someone who dares to invade her space and then later let a group of kids go through on their way to play ball. I went to sleep, full of desire for her. Lala stroked my head the next morning. I opened my eyes and followed her home. We fell asleep hoping the sun would dry our skin. The man had gone before daybreak, but he would be back. The first thing I saw were his imported leather sandals. He moved my snout with his foot to get by. Seen from below, he was a giant.

"Mitay pyra," he said, looking at the drawing on the wall.

I growled.

Lala opened her eyes.

The man stepped back. His skin was golden, his eyes green, his muscles sculpted. Such beauty irritated Lala from the outset.

"So, you're a friend of Lin . . ."

"And who are you?" Lala said.

"Don't you know who I am?"

"No."

"No?"

"No."

"You're not from here . . ."

"No."

"Ah . . ."

His smile was relieved. For a moment he thought there was a Paraguayan citizen who didn't know him. That would have been enough to destroy him, as his two loves where his fame and his name.

"Néstor Socrates."

"Sócrates?" Lala said with a look of disdain.

"Socrates, stress on the second syllable."

I jumped up to get a better look at him. I just realized who he was. He was Ofidia's owner. I had seen him in Tereré's bar. Ofidia never missed a program of *Badman*, the three o'clock soap opera. But that made for problems, because she would have a fit every time Tereré imitated him. And the latter's acting was always more convincing that Socrates's, who could barely get a line out straight. But nobody really paid any attention. All the women would fall in love with him over one stilted sentence. He even made Ofidia sigh. That's why I preferred to make room for him. While she got the hots for him, I went to the lake with Lala.

"So, you know Lin?" Lala asked him.

"Better than anyone else."

He smiled.

"I was her first boyfriend," he said in the stuck-up way of those who believe everything they touch is worth a little more. "I grew up here, right across the street from Charo's house. Lin and I would spend the whole day together. Then I . . ."

He looked for right words, staring at the ceiling.

". . . became what I am. And she stayed here."

Lala clenched her fists. The three of us knew at that moment, with the drawing looking at us from the wall, that Socrates had hurt Guayi.

"I'm having a dinner tonight. I would like to introduce you to the neighbors. It's a tradition we have here. The season begins at my house. If you'd be interested . . ."

He made a strange gesture with his hand, a mix of the flight of a bird with an arabesque, which ended up pointing to his house. Just when he was leaving, Lala realized that Socrates was her neighbor.

"At what time?"

"Nine o'clock."

"I'll be there," Lala said.

There was only one reason why she had no intention of missing that dinner: mitay pyra were two of the words Guayi repeated in her sleep.

It began to drizzle before dusk. Two uniformed maids bathed Ofidia in Socrates's garden with a French bath gel. Tereré shook with laughter in the brush. He failed to understand how a proletarian dog like me could be in love with a snooty dog. Lala was the last to show up. She walked in without asking if it was all right for me to be with her, as I left puddles of water on the cedar floor. Ofidia peered out with resignation from behind the maid. She had a pink bow around her neck and her hair was combed back with gel.

Socrates looked at Lala's tits as he received her and sent Ofidia to the kitchen. He knew I would follow her. When all is said and done, I'm a dog. We frisked around a bit by the bathroom door. Ofidia mounted me, as she was still agile in her first month of pregnancy. There were days when she liked to reverse roles. I let her, as long as no one was looking. We were busy with that when the bathroom door opened and Salma emerged, the feminine version of Socrates, with her dog Uma. Her owner's desire for stardom was fully shared by poor Uma, who kept tripping over her curls made with a curling iron and sneezing as a result of how much perfume she was wearing. Salma stood there surprised, staring at Ofidia before she shouted to Socrates to come take a look at his dog.

"She was . . . she was . . . ," she said before making some strange gestures.

In reality it was something she always wanted to do. To feel herself a man. Salma had no children and she had never had an orgasm, although when she pretended to it was the only really talented acting she did. Her mission that night was to show Socrates that one day she would be a good mother, for the way she took care of Uma. She bathed her so often she had psoriasis and her gums were swollen from having her teeth brushed so much. Socrates didn't let her finish her sentence. He put one hand on her neck, the other between her legs, and his tongue in her mouth. All so fast that Salma couldn't even blink. I left Ofidia, who growled angrily, and trotted on into the living room. In the end, Lala was all that mattered to me.

I saw her standing in a corner of the living room, cornered by two women, redheaded Swedish twins, who according to Ofidia were the stars of Paraguayan porn. They lived with the former President behind a cement wall, two houses down from Socrates. The old man had brought them home as a First World souvenir before retiring in Ypacaraí. He had abandoned politics to devote himself to fashion. He was busy organizing the next beauty contest to pick Miss Paraguay. As always in politics and fashion, his idea was to find the winner before the contest. And that night, he had found her at last. He stopped one of the maids and grabbed her chin to examine first one profile and then the other and then her full face. Without letting go, he lifted her upper lip with his little finger and examined her teeth.

"Perfect," he said.

By the end of the evening I had learned her name was Mara

and that, besides being Socrates's younger sister, she always woke up in his bed. Socrates had his grandmother, his mother, and his three sisters working in the kitchen, all dressed in uniforms, and he told all this to his guests, feigning a humility that not even he believed.

"Lala bought the lot that was for sale. She's Argentine. You've got to see how she paints. . . ," Socrates told the twins.

"Paints?" the Swedish woman who mumbled enough Spanish to repeat the last word for each sentence asked.

"She's painting murals on the walls of her house," Socrates said in a superhuman effort to make up something worth hearing. "She painted the fish boy as if she were one of the impressionists . . ."

"Impressionist?" the Swedish woman asked.

(She wasn't but an echo between Lala and Socrates.)

"Impressive," Socrates said in a husky whisper.

He had just lost himself in Lala's eyes. Once again she had bewitched someone with one moment's attention.

"Did you see him?"

"Who?"

"The fish child."

"No one saw him. It's a legend among the people of the village. They say he lives in the lake. That he guides to the deep those who drown."

He moved close to Lala as though to tell her something in confidence.

"The simple people need these things to go on living. But no one ever saw him, ever . . ."

Mara looked up from the tray of canapés, indignant over the

commentary. But her flash of anger passed when Socrates looked into her eyes.

"Tell them to serve the first course."

The storm had already begun when they served the first course. The water erased the drawings from the walls in our house. Socrates sat Lala on one side of the head of the table and Salma on the other. He served a glass of wine to each while he tried to decide with which one he would go to bed that night. The ex-President solved the matter for him when he attempted to convince him that the next queen of Paraguay was in his house. He spoke with such passion that a few minutes later, when Mara served the first course, Socrates informed her that she would leave for Asunción that very night.

"When will I come back?" Mara asked, biting her lip to keep from crying.

They told her that if everything went well she would not return. The next beauty contest, after winning in Asunción, would be in New Orleans. And after that it would only make sense for her to take up residence in Miami. He asked her to go pack her bag and wait until after dinner, because that very night she would fly to the capital.

Mara crossed the kitchen without looking at anyone, bumping into the chef, who was at that moment finishing garnishing the plates: a small pork chop, four potatoes, and two carrot triangles. It was all glazed and decorated with strands of honey. Socrates had brought him from Los Angeles the only time he had ever left the country.

"Would you like me to tell you how I discovered Socrates?" an old man seated next to Lala asked.

Socrates settled into his place, delighted to hear one more time the story of his second birth.

"At that time Socrates's name was still Pancho and he was destined to die in this village . . ."

He paused, looking at Socrates out of the corner of his eye, as though defying him to deny what he had just said. He smiled at this silence and went on: ". . . until that afternoon when I saw him rolling in the brush with that child."

The mother and the sister served the plates with a rogue smile, as though listening to a folktale. The rest of the guests began to fall silent little by little. The old man demanded their respect: he was the president of the Ypacaraí Yacht Club.

"What was her name?"

"Lin," the grandmother said without looking up from the plate she was serving Lala.

The old man looked at Salma, who was holding Uma in her arms and feeding him.

"If that child had accepted my proposal, you wouldn't be sitting there. . . . In Paraguay there's no room for two people like you. And that child had something special."

"Weren't we going to talk about me?" Socrates asked.

The old man drained his wine glass before continuing to speak.

"Socrates looked up from between the legs of the girl and saw me sitting on my catamaran, looking at them through my binoculars. I thought he was going to stop, but no. He turned so I could see them better and went back to work. . . ."

The old man sucked his chop and then gave it to Uma.

"During the following days, Socrates continued to take her to the same spot. They undressed, went for a swim in the lake, and made love on the bank. At the end of the week I had to return to Asunción because I was taping another soap opera with Rigoberti. . . . Do you remember Rigoberti?"

The members of his audience were all young. Their lives seemed to have begun yesterday. They all said no. Lala did not even move. Her stomach was churning.

"Of course not. No one remembers Rigoberti. The soap opera was going to be a failure until I saw Socrates's butt moving in the brush. The day before I left I had them come over to my house . . ."

Another pause. Uma was the only one to break the silence, crunching on a bone and swallowing the pieces. Ofidia looked at me out of the corner of her eye. She was an old fox and knew what was coming.

"I told them that they were going to be actors and that I wanted to take them with me to Asunción."

Socrates smiled, enjoying this moment in which Pancho died for ever.

"That young thing looked at you . . . ," the old man said. "Do you remember how she looked at you? She said that neither of you was going anywhere. That place was her home. Besides she had to take care of her grandfather."

He said it imitating the tone of her voice. And Lala realized that she was gripping her knife as though it were a weapon.

"Socrates didn't say a thing, but the next day he found me with his suitcase ready, all set to go. He asked me what he had to do and I told him . . ."

"'First of all, change your name,'" Socrates said, ending the tale with the words of the old man.

The audience was moved and applauded. Uma suddenly started heaving and opened her mouth in front of the old man's shoes. What she vomited up first was solid: a mound of chewed up meat with pieces of bone, all over his patent leather shoes.

"Uma, sweetheart. Are you all right?" Salma asked as she jumped up out of her seat.

The surface of the table was glass and the vomit splattered between the plates. The grandmother came running out of the kitchen with a plastic bag wrapped in her hand. She cleaned up the vomit and got out of the way so the mother could wipe the shoes with a cloth. Socrates moved his plate to hide the vomit and went on talking as though nothing had happened, trying to ignore Uma's heavings.

"A year later I came back to the village and bought this piece of land . . ."

The second time Uma threw up one of the Swedish twins made a beeline for the bathroom, covering her mouth. The third time it was liquid, pure bile, as though something inside had exploded. Salma now wouldn't even go near the dog and cried terror-struck in a corner. She knew right away that a bone had perforated the stomach of her dog.

"Take her to the doctor because she's dying," the grandmother said to Salma from the door of the kitchen.

I looked at Lala. She was thinking the same thing I was, that we were in hell. She motioned to me for us to get out of there. We ran into Mara in the garden. She was coming back from the village with her mouth all bloody and minus a few teeth. She told everyone she had fallen down. No one believed her, but the beauty contest was forgotten. And no one was surprised when the rumor began to circulate that she had paid a kid in the village to knock some of her teeth out with a rock. Lala continued walking without turning around. A few minutes later the sound of the rain could be heard again.

6

When we got home we found a tent between the four walls. Another of Charo's gifts. It still had its label. Lala opened the zipper. My moth-eaten blanket was there and the blanket with colored squares that Guayi had knit. It took her eight years to finish it, beginning when she was eight and ending the night before she left for Buenos Aires. It wasn't because she was lazy, but because she knitted a square color for everything important that happened. Lala wrapped herself up in the blanket and cried herself to sleep. That was something else that was different since we had arrived. Now she cried, almost every night, and for no reason, just like Guayi. It wasn't because she was sad. It was just that she needed to cry in order to fall asleep. We were busy with that, crossing the border into dreamland, when Socrates unzipped the tent a few centimeters. It was still raining outside with the same fury and it was beginning to leak inside. I dreamt that the drops of water were Lala's tears.

"What do you want," Lala said, sticking her head out from under the blankets.

"Uma died at the veterinarian's."

Lala covered her head again and her face was swollen from crying so hard. She couldn't think of a thing to say.

"I want you to come sleep at my house. I have a guest room."

"I'm fine here."

"You're going to get soaked here. Water's starting to come in."

"I like the water."

Socrates nodded his head. Lala's answer left him without any reply.

"You left without saying goodbye to her," Lala said.

"What?"

"I said you left without saying goodbye to her."

Socrates came into the tent and sat down next to me.

"What was I going to tell her?" he asked her.

Socrates did not look at her, but Lala was looking at him. She wanted to hurt him.

"She never spoke to me about you."

"No?"

"Never."

"She worked in your house."

Lala nodded.

"You were going to build this house together."

Lala nodded again.

"But she remained in Buenos Aires."

He looked at her now. And suddenly, almost without taking a breath, he began to cry. Not like a man, but crying like a child whose favorite toy has been taken away.

"I can't get her out of my mind. I can't. I tell myself every night that she was just like all the others in the village. But she comes to me in my dreams. . . . And the fact is that I barely like women . . . But I realized something tonight, when the others had gone . . ."

He looked at Lala surprised, because he was telling the truth and couldn't believe it.

"I was never happy again. From the day I left her, I was never happy again. Anyone listening to me would think I am mad. I have everything anyone could want, fame, sex, money . . . but the one thing I want, when all is said and done, is to roll in the hay again with her. I want her to kiss me, to suck me, to bite me . . ."

He wiped the snot away with his shirt sleeve. And at that moment Lala began to like Socrates.

"Do you know what she used to do?" he asked smiling through the snot and tears. "She would gather up abandoned bird's eggs she would find. . . . She would ask me to put them inside her. She would say, 'Here inside I have room for them all. . . . Why should they be orphans?'"

Lala remembered Guayi's caresses inside her in the warm water of the bathtub.

"There's something else . . ." Socrates said. "She was pregnant. She told me the last night I saw her. She didn't beg for me to stay and took for granted I wasn't going to leave her. She wasn't surprised nor afraid. She was radiant. I was convinced she was lying and making it up. But deep down I knew she was right."

I looked at Lala, but she didn't even look at me.

"Did she have it?"

"I don't know. They said she was pregnant. But no one saw the baby. And they never heard it cry. Although there were those in the village who said . . ."

"What did they say?"

". . . People always talk . . ."

"What did they say?"

"That they saw her swimming in the lake, with a baby."

The rain continued to fall and Lala did not look at Socrates. Instead, she looked at the drawing of the fish child; the water had made part of the carbon ink run until it reached the cement floor.

"You never saw her again?"

"I came back the following summer to find her. But she had already gone to Buenos Aires."

Lala recalled the stretch marks Guayi had on her tummy, below her ribs, the only marks on a skin so taut that it looked like leather.

"Were you fat at one time?" she had asked her the first time she saw her naked, running the tip of her finger over her.

"Before I met you?"

"What did you look like?"

"Old. Before I met you I was old."

That's what Guayi said, and she was the one now working the tip of her tongue, so lightly that Lala forgot those marks. But they were there, like the sign of a body that had had another shape. Lala left the house and walked down to the dock. She didn't even turn around when Socrates warned her that it was no night to be near the lake. At the dock, I jumped into the boat before Lala could draw away without me. I dug my nails into the boards and paid no attention to her shouting for me to get out. Finally she started rowing toward the middle and each pull on the oar was a blow that seemed to slash the water. She uttered something with each blow, unconnected, angry words. A child? Guayi? Why hadn't she said anything? And where was that child now? She talked to the foam of the water whipped up by the storm, and the possibility, just the possibility, that the child was alive beneath the waves, was destroying her world just as fast as the water was coming into the boat, rocking it from one side to the other, until in one of the turns Lala let the water take her with it. The force turned the canoe over and suddenly the lake was larger than the world. The wind was impelling along both clouds and waves, turning my barking into bubbles. The lighthouse disappeared, along with the shoreline and the house. I opened my mouth and my lungs filled with water. Lala continued to swim toward the bottom, searching for him, until she ran out of breath. . . . And I was going to go with her, even if she tried to kick me away. A couple of strokes were enough to show her that I was going to follow her to the end. . . . And that must have been what made her change her mind, because just when my body started to go limp, I saw her, her hair swirling around all over the place, framed in bubbles, embracing me, paddling toward the surface. Charo was waiting for us. The storm seemed to have blown over and was fading, leaving behind a freezing rain. He wrapped Lala in a blanket and handed her his bottle of brandy while he rowed toward the shore.

"Why didn't you tell me?" Lala asked.

"Mbay nde nderein cheve."

"Speak to me in Spanish."

"Because you didn't ask me."

Lala took a drink of the brandy, took off the blanket and put it over my shoulders before asking him again.

"Why didn't you tell me she had a child?"

Charo stopped rowing and sat looking at Socrates's house.

"During the first months she followed his life on TV. The fourth month she turned the TV off and began to spend her days in the water. I told her it wasn't good for the baby. But she had no doubts and knew what she had to do.

The old man put his hands in the water and dampened his neck.

"One night I found her filling the bathtub with buckets of water. I asked her what she was doing and she told me that it had to be born in there. She was in the seventh month of pregnancy. She asked me to open the window so the moonlight came in and for me to help her get undressed. When she got into the water a contraction made her sit down in pain.

The old man took the brandy from her and drank it down, looking at her over the edge of the bottle.

"It was born at one in the morning. Its eyes were so clear as to look white. Lin took it out of the water to embrace it. The baby did not cry. It opened its mouth as if to cry, but no sound came out. In a few seconds it started to gasp for air. Lin looked at me. Then, without a word, she put it back in the water. She held its body . . . like this . . . until the baby opened its eyes . . . and the mouth . . . and breathed."

The old man did not cry. Neither did Lala. I was the only one who couldn't stand it.

"That first night we watched it swim. My granddaughter got in the bathtub a couple of times to embrace it and to let it nurse. But by morning something was wrong and it began to lie still at the bottom of the water, as though it wasn't getting enough air. Lin asked me to look after it and left. She came back with an air compressor and a tube . . . the kind that fishbowls have to oxygenate the water."

Lala nodded.

"She had given the veterinarian the TV in exchange for it. She asked me to take it to him, because she didn't want him to come there. In reality she never allowed anyone back in the house. Still, people had begun to talk. Some believed it had died at childbirth and we had buried it out in back. And that Lin had gone mad, which is why she never left the house. One night some kids opened the window and saw her laughing, looking at the water. She was laughing because the baby already recognized her and was beginning to smile. After that they never left us alone. The veterinarian told his wife about the tub. The kids told their friends about the bathtub. By the end of the week the whole town was whispering that we had a monster locked up in the house. . . . Do you see this scar I have here?"

He touched a mark that he had above his eyebrow.

"One day they pelted me with rocks when I came out of the supermarket. I never told Lin. Nor did I tell her that some newspaper reporters and the owner of a circus and a Belgian scientist who was vacationing in Ypacaraí showed up. I didn't have to. Lin understood everything. She helped me cover the windows with sheets of wood. She knew we were running out of time. The baby was getting big and the bathtub was smaller and smaller. After five months it stopped nursing overnight. The two got sick together and didn't eat or sleep . . ."

The old man paused and looked at the lake.

"One morning she asked me to help her bring it here. She went into the water with the baby. They swam together until nightfall. And when I helped her get back in the canoe, the baby wasn't with her."

7

Charo showed her that night the letters he had received from his granddaughter. They were written in Guaraní and sent from where she was being held. "You once asked me not to lie to you and I'm not going to lie to you. I lost my job. I did things wrong. I'm calmer now. I'm going to pay for what I did. Not for what they think I did, but only for what you and I know about," the first letter said, which the old man translated with difficulty, as though Guaraní and Spanish did not match. "I dreamed that the room where I sleep is full of water. All the girls who are sleeping with me are drowning. There are thirteen of them. Fourteen, counting me. When no one is left he comes to look for me. He parts the bars on the windows as though they were algae. He swims in, takes my hand, and leads me away with him. The room isn't the only place that filled with water. The whole world is in the bottom of the lake. The sky is the surface, but you can't raise your head above it to breathe. And there's no one left. Just him and me." Lala is only mentioned at the end: "A friend is going to show up looking for me. Let her use my room. Let her wait for me. Help her pick out a lot, which must be facing the lake." One order after another. That wasn't the Guayi we knew. The second letter took it for granted that we had arrived in Ypacaraí. "Is she

still there? Did she get what I sent? Is she building the house?"
The third letter arrived along with the second, and the fourth a
day after. She wrote one after the other. She had been in deten-
tion three weeks and the old man already had a box full of letters.
She repeated the same thing in all of them, which was that Lala
wasn't to be told a thing. Not that she was detained nor that she
knew she was there. But Guayi's time span was always very short,
as though her desire could not be contained in time and space.
Her enthusiasm began to wither from one letter to the next. She
didn't sound good in the last one and she no longer asked about
Lala. They were fewer and far between and shorter. Until one day
there were no more. The old man had counted them. There were
thirty letters. Not one more and not one less. Thirty days and his
granddaughter had let the past and the future go. He refolded the
letters and put them away, one by one, in their envelopes.

Lala bit her lip as she watched him without saying a word. It
wasn't his fault. His granddaughter had asked him not to tell her.
Thirty days, she repeated without opening her mouth. Thirty days
locked up with her here, swimming in Lake Ypacaraí. She left the
house and walked for hours. Tiring herself out was the only thing
that calmed her. At dawn she returned to her house on the lake
and found the workers having something hot to eat before beginning their work. It had stopped raining but the drizzle was still
falling slantwise because of the wind.

"Come see this," the foreman told her.

He took her to the back of the lot. Ofidia was giving birth
among the rubble. Lala looked at me sideways, because she knew
they were mine. The first three had been born. They were
squeaking like mice and they were ugly, very ugly. The fourth was

stillborn. Ofidia shoved him aside with her snout and continued to lick the ones that were alive. The last thing to come out was the placenta. Lala gave it to Ofidia so she could eat it. The foreman was kneeling down beside them, watching the spectacle while crunching a cracker with his gums.

"Eva was born today," he said.

"Who?"

"Eva. The first baby in history to be cloned. A caesarean, in the United States. From the mother's own cells. They say that three more babes are going to be born this week from the cells their parents saved from their children who died."

The foreman stood up and went back to work. Lala picked up the dead puppy. Its body was still warm. She buried it in the back of the lot before going back to talk to the workers. She was going to be gone for a while, she told them, but Charo would be in charge. Her decision didn't surprise the old man.

"He can go with you if you want, but if he shits you have to clean it up. If he's asphyxiated the company bears no blame," the bus driver said that same afternoon, after attempting to remove me forcibly, trying in vain to entice me with food, yelling at me and hitting me. All in vain. I dug my claws in and wouldn't budge. The only way to win in the human world is to wear them down.

Lala forgot to take me off when we stopped. She wasn't at her best. Nor did she move from her seat. She neither ate nor stretched her legs during the thirty-two hours of the trip. She got up once to go to the bathroom, washing the bitterness from her mouth with a mouthful of water. When they opened the doors in Retiro Station, I had peed all over myself and I could barely open my eyes for the light. The driver had to put up with the complaints of the passengers in silence. He took his revenge by looking at her ass as she wiped the luggage compartment down with a rag and even made her spray the place with room freshener before returning the bag I was in to her.

Lala crossed the terminal to the platform facing north. The bum she left the keys to the Mercedes with a few months before was sleeping in the same position in one of the doorways. The only thing new was a sculpture exhibit: dinosaurs made from scrap metal. Lala stopped suddenly in the middle of the central hall, which obliged several passengers to curse her as they went around her. An immobile body in their midst broke the harmony of the ant hill. She looked at the doors that she could go out of, the platforms that would take her even farther, and even the skylights, as though considering the possibility of flying away. Guayi did not specify in her letters which institute she was in. She felt the impact of someone bumping into her from behind, pushing her toward the platforms. It was a young kid running off among the legs of the tyrannosaurus with someone's purse. She used this shove to continue walking toward the platform facing north. Something as accidental as the shove of a pickpocket could decide her destiny at that moment.

We traveled in the bicycle car, Lala with her head glued to the window, trying to see the city. But it was already dark and all she could see was her own reflection. She didn't like what she saw.

She had become ugly without Guayi to look at her. There suddenly appeared among the people reflected in the window someone she knew. A school chum, the son of the former Minister of Economy, the one who had fled the country. He was sweating in a suit that was too small for him. Lala looked away, turning her back to him. But he had already recognized her and made his way over to her, breaking the precarious silence of the passengers jammed together like sardines.

"Lala. . . . Is that you?"

She considered the option of saying no, denying at any cost who she was. But the guy was already hugging her, while Lala tried to remember his name. Something with an o . . . Pocho . . . Mocho . . .

"Rocho?"

They had never been friends. Not he or anyone else in her whole class. The first couple of years they treated her as though she were weird. Then as someone who has crazy, queer, a lesbo. . . . And now there he was clutching her hand with his eyes filled with anger, telling her: "I called you a couple of times . . . We all called you . . . We went to the burial . . . Your aunt told us you left the same night as that bitch . . ."

The bitch was Guayi. Evidently we were the last ones to find out that they had accused her of Brontë's death.

"Everything you guys did for her . . . Ungrateful bitch . . . In any case she's rotting in jail . . . I know what I'm telling you. I'm going to be a lawyer in a couple of years. In this country it's better to die than go to jail . . ."

She liked seeing him fat, bald, and wearing a wedding ring on his finger.

"We always talk about you on birthdays. . . . You're . . ."

Unrecognizable. Rocho paused to get a good look at her. His main role in the next birthday party depended on it, on the details. Her face was tanned by sun and dust, a man's clothes, her hair chopped close in back by scissors.

"I called your aunt to invite you to the graduation party, but she told me she still had no word from you . . ."

"I was traveling."

"I thought so. When you didn't return to school we guessed that you had to get away. Where did you go?"

"Paraguay."

"Paraguay? Of course, the place doesn't matter . . . what you needed was to be far away. It must have been real difficult . . . to be left without a thing overnight . . ."

Lala looked at him in stony-faced silence. Rocho had no intention of giving up without a struggle.

"My birthday is Friday. Everyone's going to be there. Why don't you come?"

"I'm not staying in Buenos Aires."

Rocho looked at the floor trying to find something else to say. Then he saw that Lala was wearing sandals, even though it was almost winter. She didn't seem to feel the cold.

"Are you all right?" he asked Lala with a concern so genuine he even surprised himself.

"No."

"Ah . . ."

Pause.

"Are you all right?" she asked him.

"I can't complain. I'm doing lower-division courses at the University of Buenos Aires, I bought a car, I'm going to have a child . . ."

The train stopped at a station. Rocho stopped ticking things off and rapidly took a card out of his pocket.

"I've been told that the trial is held up because of a lack of evidence. I'm working in my family's firm. . . . If you need any help, call us."

He took a step back. He got off the car and stood there looking at her while the doors closed.

8

It was eight o'clock on a winter evening, without any moon. Time to take the garbage out to the street. Two maids on one of the corners were taking the chance to gossip while they put their bags out on the sidewalk. Lala recognized one of them. It was Chapulina, one of Guayi's friends. The one who got her the job when she arrived in Buenos Aires. Chapulina also recognized her, because she stopped laughing when she saw her cross through one of the circles of lights the streetlights cast on the cobblestone street. She followed her with her eyes until Lala disappeared in the dark.

A minute later Lala rang the door to her house. She had no choice, since her keys no longer worked. The lock wasn't the only thing that had been changed. Now the house was painted a pastel yellow with white shutters, as though they had wanted to wash its face. There was hysterical barking from the other side of the door, so high-pitched it made your teeth hurt. The maid asked who it was twice before opening the door. Lala repeated her name. The second time she opened the door a few centimeters, without removing the chain. A ridiculous Pekinese showed its face, growling at me so furiously that drool was hanging from its teeth.

"Are you looking for someone?"

Lala didn't answer. She just stood there looking at her. She was wearing one of Guayi's uniforms. The maid looked at the two of us with the same coldness. We were no longer a girl and her dog from Acassuso.

"We don't have anything to give you . . ." she said, looking at the security guard who was hurrying over.

Guayi was wrong. She told Lala that you could always tell she was from the neighborhood. Lala backed away. The best thing she could do was leave. Then she heard laughing from the living room and she recognized her aunt's laugh.

"I'm looking for Felicitas."

"Madam is busy. . . . Who's looking for her?"

"Her niece."

"Wait here."

Lala stood standing in front of the door, feeling the look of the security guard on the back of her neck. She heard in the silence of the night the maid say her name. Then the scrape of a chair being pushed back. And there was Felicitas, as plastic looking as always. With her starched clothes, her hair bleached blond, her mask of makeup.

"Hello, Aunt Felicitas."

Felicitas raised her hand to her mouth. She liked melodrama. She always brought Lala Corín Tellado novels to family reunions. And once she invited us to her house to see *The Bird Sings Itself to Death*. When we arrived, there was a bowl of popcorn on the table and a pack of Kleenex on each chair for the tears.

"Where . . . ? Why . . . ? I thought that . . ."

Felicitas caressed her head and slowly rested it on her shoulder. Lala put up with it by biting her lip. She saw her aunt's friends standing a few meters away.

"Where did you go?" she finally said.

"Paraguay."

Felicitas looked Lala up and down and then one part at a time. Her skin was wrinkled. Her fingernails and hair were dirty. She didn't smell good.

"Are you hungry?"

"Yes."

She told the maid: "Prepare a plate of food for her."

She started to shut the door, but Lala stuck her foot out so I could come in.

"He's with me."

She guided Lala into the dining room by her shoulder. She had had the furniture moved around down to the last piece. The only family photo left was on top of the piano. Lala stopped to look at it. Felicitas had taken it on someone's birthday. She made them huddle into each other and smile at the same time, for the first and last time. You could see how uncomfortable they were in the corners of their mouths.

"I knew you would be back. That's what I told everyone. Everyone handles these things in his own way. The inspector in charge of the case, Inspector Mastrangelo, a charming man, so attentive, such a hard worker. . . . The Inspector is convinced that you saw something that night and that's why you left, in a state of shock. He put your picture out everywhere, even on television, even with the gas bills, just like in the United States. I never lost hope, nor did Mastrangelo. We've got to call him, don't we? Lala?"

Lala couldn't help seeing Brontë's hand resting on her shoulder.

"Sweetheart . . . do you want to take a bath before you eat?"

"No."

She ate without taking her eyes off the plate, almost without breathing between mouthfuls.

"Take it slow, Lala. You're going to get sick," one of the women said.

"Drink a little bit of water," another said, shoving the glass on the table toward her with a sculpted fingernail.

"What day does Chapulina have off?" Lala asked her.

"What?"

"What day doesn't she work?"

The fingernail exchanged glances with Felicitas, not understanding.

"Tuesdays."

"Tomorrow."

"Yes, tomorrow."

"What time does she get off?"

"Lala . . . what difference does it make?"

"What time does she get off?" Lala asked again.

"Whenever she wants. Generally, she leaves at seven or eight to take advantage of the day."

Felicitas got up from the table.

"Girls, we'll leave dessert for another day. . . . Let me show you out."

They had no choice but to follow her, although no one

wanted to leave, now that something was happening. Lala was left alone at the table. She opened a window, lit one of the butts from the ashtray and leaned back in a chair. The maid came in with dessert.

"What's your name?"

"Elizabeth, but they call me Betty."

"You're not from here . . ."

"No, I'm from Uruguay, from Chui. . . . Your aunt hired me when she came to live in this house. It seems that the one who was here before . . ."

Betty made a gesture indicating theft with such elegance that it seemed more like a magic act than anything else.

"I'm sorry I didn't recognize you. . . . You would like me to fix you a bath?"

"I can do it."

"I can, too."

She followed Betty upstairs. She was looking at her from behind, trying to imagine it was Guayi's body moving itself in that pink uniform. But it wasn't the same thing. It was never going to be the same thing. When she saw Betty kneeling in front of the bathtub, checking the temperature of the water, she realized she wasn't going to be able to spend more than one night in that house. She couldn't stand being there without Guayi.

"Go to bed, Betty," Felicitas said from the doorway.

Betty left saying goodnight.

"Don't say much to her. She's a real parrot. Anything you tell her tomorrow, the whole Northside will know it."

Lala smiled. Her aunt's world ended at the General Paz highway. Lala lowered her panties and sat down on the toilet to pee.

"Your mother called two days ago. She was making a retreat to a Buddhist temple in Bombay, which is why she didn't call before. . . . But she knows everything, poor thing. She couldn't stop crying. . . . She's over there singing to Sai Baba." She shrugged her shoulder. "Nobody says it better than Coelho: 'Everyone struggles with his guilt.' Are you all right? Do you want to talk?"

"About what?"

"About that night, sweetheart. . . . What happened that night? You must have seen something to disappear like that. . . . Listen to me, Lala . . . You can tell me anything. . . . I know the two of you were friends . . . but you can't try to defend her. . . . They caught up with her at the station with a ticket in her purse. Everything was gone from the house. Your mother's jewels, furniture, even paintings. . . . Everybody knows your father went downhill when your mother left. That kid must have got to him . . . she got to him and started to sell everything . . ."

"I'm the one who sold all the stuff. She had nothing to do with it."

Felicitas opened her mouth to go on talking, and just then, just as Lala was starting to undress, she grasped what she had just heard.

"You? Why would you sell . . . ?"

She dropped the sentence and stood staring at Lala.

"If she didn't do a thing, your father . . . who . . . ?"

"I did it. I did him a favor. He would never have had the courage."

Pause.

Lala held her look while unbuttoning the shirt she was wearing. Felicitas was the first to lower her gaze.

The only friend Lala had when we lived here, the trainer, worked at a dog school next to Los Chinos, the slum where Pep took me every night. She met him one day when she hid in the bed of the truck to see where we were going. But instead of following her brother, Lala stood there looking at the trainer, on the other side of the grillwork, on his landfill property on the river. She saw him shout, raise his hand, and take the attack of a Sheepdog who hung stuck to him while he twisted him around in the air. If he hadn't been wearing an aluminum sleeve, we would have thought the dog was attacking him. But the minute he lowered his arm, the dog started wagging his tail waiting for his treat. When we came out of the hut, we found the two of them taking a smoke in the bed of the truck. That day the trainer told her one of the keys for controlling dogs: the last one to avert his gaze is the one who is in charge. The one who draws the line.

Felicitas was checking the bathroom tiles as though they were a labyrinth.

"Listen to what I'm about to tell you. I don't want you to repeat that stupidity. The case is closed. People have forgotten all about it. This family has gone through enough without our having to relive a scandal . . ."

"What family?"

"What do you mean, what family?" Felicitas said, who was beginning to get the idea that her niece was less and less of this world. "Your family, Lala . . ."

"There's no family left."

Lala went on getting undressed. It was the only way to be left alone.

"If you're all mixed up we can talk to the psychiatrists who are taking care of Pep. You could even stay at the clinic for a while where he is. . . . They take both men and women. . . . It's near here, in San Isisdro . . . They have a darling garden and it's painted all white on the inside . . ."

Felicitas backed away as Lala's state of undress progressed.

"Let's do this . . . Take a bath, go to bed . . . in the morning, all fresh, we'll talk about everything . . ."

She closed the bathroom door. Lala felt dizzy, her skin burning. The water was boiling. When she stuck her head in, the water overflowed the edges.

Felicitas had turned Lala's room into a guest room. The new decor followed the same logic as the rest of the house, with the walls painted and the furniture moved. A woman's pajama under the pillow on the left, a man's pajama under the pillow on the right. Lala put on the man's top, closed the door to look at herself in the mirror, and passed her hand over her shorn head. Her eyes were large when she wore her hair long and now, without hair or eyebrows, they made her look like those animated Japanese cartoon characters.

"Do you like it?"

She smiled at me from the mirror.

"I like it."

She had found the pair of scissors, the tweezers, and the shaver in a wicker basket among the gels and creams. She plucked her eyebrows one by one, continued with the scissors, and then ran the razor over her head.

"Do you think she's going to like it?"

It always bothered her that Guayi would tell her she had a classic look, taking it as an insult. She turned the light off and left the room. The floor tiles of the kitchen were cold. She felt the chill spread through her bare feet and climb her legs. She could see herself lying there, entwined with Guayi. She went over to Betty's door and pushed it open with her finger. She was sleeping with her eyes half-open and snoring softly. But she opened her eyes after a few minutes, as though she had felt someone else was in the room.

"Miss . . ."

"I'm sorry. I didn't mean to wake you up."

Lala started to shut the door, but Betty stopped her.

"Hold on. I have something for you."

She got up and searched one the drawers of her dresser until she found what she was looking for. It was a photograph, with Lala staring into the camera. Her lips half-parted, her hair slicked back on her head. Lala had to sit down on the bed to look at the photo. Never, in all these months, had she felt more strongly Guayi's absence. She saw her on top of her in that same bed, climbing up her body until she looked in her eyes.

"This is the face I want," she had said reaching for the camera she had ready on the nightstand.

Guayi wanted her picture, but only the face. She had begged her for it for months. She said there was a moment, a very brief moment, in which she was transformed. She wanted to show her, wanted her to see it. And she was right, because she was never happier than that day.

"It was in the bottom of the drawer. I don't know how it ended up there. The police turned everything upside down and took some stuff with them. Your aunt told me to throw the rest of the stuff away. She didn't want anything left. I found the photograph last month straightening things up. . . . Now today, when I saw you, I realized that it was you. You don't look like the photograph that is in the living room."

Pep's room was where Felicitas stored things she took out of circulation. Lala recognized a windbreaker sticking out of a garbage bag and emptied the bag on the bed. She found a school uniform, a taekwondo outfit, ski clothes, a girl's pair of underpants. That's how her aunt had been waiting for her, with her clothes in garbage bags.

The key to the terrace was in the same place as always. Not by accident, since no one had touched the garden during the last months. The weeds had taken over, but some resistant things could be seen, like some of the hot peppers Pep had brought from Mexico, tomatoes, cilantro, some sprigs of rosemary, lemon balm, mint. The ground was covered with dried tomatoes and peppers. They grew without anybody caring and dried up the same way. Lala began to pull the weeds. It was the only time she liked her brother, when she saw him tending his garden as though his life depended on five meters of ground. She cleared the undergrowth from a circle, enough room for her and me. She cleared the ground with her hand and sat down to watch the dawn. Only then, on the damp ground, was she able to fall asleep.

We were awakened by the barking of the schizophrenic Pekinese. Disoriented, Lala opened her eyes and sat down on the terrace. She remembered where we were when she saw the neighbor's pool instead of the lake. She grabbed the Pekinese by the neck and held him over the void that stretched back to the garden.

"Are you going to shut up?"

She always woke up in a bad mood. You've got to tiptoe around her for the first hour. The Pekinese opened his eyes wide, scrunched up his legs and hindquarters and let go with a thin stream of pee.

"That's better. I'm going to let you off this time. . . . But I don't want to hear you again, understand?"

She stared him in the eyes until the Pekinese looked away. Then she set him down on the terrace. The Pekinese didn't let out a peep. He walked away slowly without barking, his tail between his legs.

"You too, get up . . ."

See what I mean?

I followed her in silence to her room. She put on the clothes that she had found the night before in the garbage bags. The checkered skirt from her school uniform, a ski turtleneck, Pep's lace-ups, and a leather jacket she and Guayi had bought at a used clothing store. Felicitas was in Brontë's study when she saw her go out. She had gotten up early to call the clinic where Pep was.

"No, it's not about him, but about his sister. Yes, she showed up, but she's not well. . . . I need for you to see her right away today, but I don't know if she will want to . . . ," the bitch was saying when I went by the study door. "I would prefer for you to come and give me a hand. . . . Yes, right now . . ."

When she saw Lala open the front door, she set the phone on the table and ran down the stairs. Lala heard her aunt shout and turned around at the end of the block. Felicitas looked at her with terror. There wasn't a hair left on her head.

"Where are you going?"

"For a walk."

"Why don't you wait a second for me? I'll change and we'll go together . . ."

"When I get back we'll go together."

"How long will that be?"

"Not long."

"How long?"

"Half an hour."

Felicitas nodded.

"I'll be waiting for you."

"Wait for me," Lala said.

And she disappeared around the hedge. She crossed the street whistling her school song. At the end of the block she turned around.

"Say goodbye, Serafín. It's the last time you'll see this house."

10

"Do you remember me?"

Lala's voice startled her. It was eight o'clock on a freezing morning. Lala had spent the last hour making shapes with the breath from her mouth every time she exhaled forcefully. The cold felt like pins jabbing her shorn head. It was the first thing Chapulina saw. The cold had turned her skin blue.

"I'm sorry. I startled you."

Chapulina didn't say a thing. She stared at her uneasily, trying to decide what to say and what not to say.

"You know who I am, right?"

"Of course I do. You haven't changed that much. . . . Madam says you're like someone else. All she does is talk about you after last night . . ."

Chapulina saw me standing behind Lala.

"I recognized you yesterday because of the dog. . . . Then I thought it couldn't be you. If you'd been gone all this time, why would you come back now . . . ?"

"I didn't know what was going on here. That's why I didn't come back."

Chapulina began to walk toward the station. Cars started to go by with their windows rolled up and the heat on full blast to melt the thin layer of frost covering the windows.

"Are you going to the station?" Lala asked her.

"Yes."

"Can I walk with you?"

"If you want . . ."

"Do you still live in Tigre?"

Chapulina looked at her out of the side of her eyes and nodded. Her interest bothered her. They walked a whole block without speaking. Until finally Lala couldn't stand it any more.

"Do you see her?"

"I used to, but not now. She asked me not to go anymore."

They stopped to let a school bus by.

"Where is she?"

"In La Plata. In an institute for minors."

"And how do I get there?"

The station appeared around the corner. But Chapulina wasn't moving. She stopped abruptly and looked Lala in the eyes for the first time.

"She doesn't want anyone to go see her."

"I don't care. I'm going anyway."

"You'll just complicate things."

"How?"

"Just because."

"All I want to know is what happened . . ."

"You don't know?"

"No."

Chapulina looked at her without saying a word. She didn't believe her, but it didn't matter. She said hello to a newspaper boy who went by, peddling standing up on his bike. She felt uneasy and didn't like being seen with her. She had already gotten into enough of a mess by being Guayi's friend. Best end it once and for all and get on with her own business.

"Guayi never told me what happened that night. Not me and not the lawyer they assigned her and not the judge. She wouldn't open her mouth. Not even when the judge told her that if she wouldn't speak in her own defense she was going to be declared guilty. She only spoke once, when they asked her about her connection to you . . ."

"What did she say?"

"That you had nothing to do with it."

Chapulina stared at Lala. Even today she was convinced her friend had lied. The whole room thought the same thing, even the judge. But the silence of the accused left the lawyer no other choice but to do what he did.

"A week later madam came home all excited. She had just found out at the gym that Guayi had been found guilty. She made me open a bottle of cider to go celebrate with your aunt. Her husband was also happy because, for once, justice had been done in this country and things were getting better. Guayi was taken the next day to the Institute in La Plata. The first time I went to see her, she told me they were going to transfer her to another Institute in Buenos Aires, that there were too many girls there, and there weren't enough beds to go around. But in the end she stayed there, until she turns eighteen . . ."

"That's only a month away."

"Yes. In a month they'll take her to Ezeiza Airport."

The train was approaching, blowing its horn. Chapulina started to walk away, but Lala grabbed her by the arm.

"Tell me how to get there."

"You've never gone to La Plata?"

"No."

"Go to Constitution Station and take the train there to La Plata. . . . You know where Constitution is, right?"

Even before she asked she knew she didn't. She would never understand the girls from the North End. She took some eyeliner out of her pocket, grabbed Lala's hand, and wrote down how to get there, including the name of the Institute.

"OK, now you can't get lost . . . ," she said without looking at Lala, running toward the station.

Until she met Guayi, Lala had only gone into the city to go to the doctor's or take care of some business. She hated the theater, Florida Street, and Corrientes Avenue. She had never gone dancing. She preferred to stay in her room reading a comic book than to go to one of the hangouts in San Isidro where her fellow students liked to go. Guayi, on the other hand, liked to dance and party.

"If you won't come with me, I'll screw the first guy who looks at me," she told Lala one Saturday afternoon.

Her day off started at noon, but she had spent the afternoon trying to convince Lala to go with her to a dive where her cousin worked as a bouncer. They could spend the night in Moreno and return the next day.

"All you have to do is move your butt. I've got dresses for both of us in my bag . If you want you can even bring . . . ," she said, looking at me. "My cousin'll pick us up at the station and he can stay with him at the door to the place."

She finally convinced her. Lala had no interest in seeing Moreno. She was no more interested in the slums than she was in the sex scene and was happy with her lack of experience. If she agreed to go, it was because she knew Guayi wasn't lying. If she wouldn't go with her that night, she'd have ended up in some guy's bed. The cousin was waiting for us a couple of hours later at the station. Cousin, which is how he asked Lala to call him, looked like he was about to burst as a consequence of the quantity of anabolics he had consumed in the past decade. His hair came down to his waist and he wore it loose. His voice produced a paralyzing effect, because it was high and thin. He had begun to take anabolics to change his voice. In the end it changed him completely, all except for his voice.

"Tell me you like it . . ."

That was the first thing he said to Guayi. He had ironed his hair with cream.

"It was curly until last week," he explained to Lala.

Guayi told him the truth—it looked terrible—and went to change in the bathroom of the station. There was no way to convince Lala to put on a dress, not even to have a good time. Before dawn she was standing out by the door with us.

"You're not dancing anymore," Long-Hair asked her. "Don't you like the cumbia?"

"More or less."

"And Guayi?"

"Leading the pack."

"Waving her tee-shirt in the air?"

"Something like that."

Cousin frisked two men who let him do it, their arms in the air.

"Go on in."

The guys went in. Lala stood there looking at a girl vomiting on the corner. Cousin leaned against the wall.

"She's going to break your heart."

"I know."

Guayi came out at dawn. She was completely drunk. Her lips were swollen from all the kisses she had passed out in there.

"Come on . . . Now I want to dance with you," she told Lala.

Two hours later, when they exited in the tide of survivors, Lala was also drunk. She even snored on the trip back. The city ceased to be hostile with Guayi at her side. It turned into some-place where, if you were sleepy, you could sleep.

11

The Institute for minors was located on one of the many diagonals in La Plata. It was a white monster, gigantic and dirty even from seven blocks away. Lala stopped to look at it. Something had begun to collapse since we had come back. From far way, she had invented a world in which there was no room for the past. All she had were memories of Guayi and the rest had disappeared. Neighborhood, home, school, family. Above all her family and above all Brontë.

Last night, before going into Pep's room, I saw her standing in the same spot where I'd found Brontë two months before. She was barefoot and running her foot along the carpet with a barely perceptible movement, like a cat. Felicitas had left everything in the same place and Lala didn't touch a thing. She ran her finger around the edge of the desk, over his pens, his ashtray, his papers, even all the keys of his typewriter. She struck one after the other. She wrote an invisible hello that remained imprinted on the machine's roller.

"Lin Guaiyen . . . Guai-yen . . . No, she's not Japanese. She's Paraguayan," Lala said to the guard she talked to at the Institute. "She's been here for two months . . ."

She held her breath as she watched him check the list of inmates. She still thought it could all be a mistake. From the other end of the counter, a redhead guard looked up from the gossip magazine she was reading. She was curious about Lala and had no intention of hiding it.

"She's here. . . . The problem is they wrote her name wrong and she's under Gayen . . ."

"Change it."

"No, it stays that way. I already explained it to the last person who came to see your friend. If they sent her over from the court as Gayen, she's Gayen for the rest of her life."

She was serious.

"Who was that?" Lala asked.

"What?"

"The last person who came to see her. Who was it?"

"I have no idea. I have the list of last month's visits and no one came last month."

He breathed with a whistle, like an asthmatic or a smoker. His teeth were stained.

"Look, you have about a half hour before the end of visiting hours."

"That's all right."

"I'm going to have to frisk you."

Lala agreed. The guard struggled to get up, but the redhead beat him to it.

"Let me."

She told Lala to come over.

She came out from behind the counter and walked along a corridor to the screening room. Everything was big about her, her eyes, hands, mouth, boobs, ass. . . . She looked like an extra from a cheap porno film, disguised by her uniform. I followed Lala in before she could shut the door. It was a tiny room, bare except for a bed in one corner and a metal cabinet from which the redhead took out a box of latex gloves.

"The mutt's with you?"

The mutt was me.

"Yes."

"What's his name?"

"Serafín."

She smiled, thinking it was a joke.

"Take your pants off. And tell the little angel he better not shit or pee."

Lala undressed without taking her eyes off the floor, while the guard emptied her bag out on the bed. She followed with her clothes, checking the pockets, the inside of the lace-ups and, finally, Lala's body.

"Spread your legs. You know how this works, right?"

Lala nodded again, while the redhead put a latex glove on her left hand. She had no idea. She didn't even blink when she felt the guard's hand checking her and lingering inside her a second longer than was necessary.

"So then, you've come to see Gayen . . . Are you a friend of hers?"

"No. Her lover."

The redhead looked up and smiled, without removing her hand.

"She didn't tell me she had a lover."

Lala held her gaze.

"Get dressed. I'll wait for you outside."

She tossed the glove in the wastebasket and left us alone. Lala remained sitting on the cot. A minute later the redhead opened the door to the visitor's yard with a ring of keys.

"She's not here . . . I'm going to get her for you now . . ."

She thrust her into the yard and locked the door again. It was the airshaft of the Institute. An airshaft of cement and metal without a shred of greenery, intoxicating in its smell of fear, piss, and adrenaline. Girls of different ages were looking out of some of the barred windows. They threw gum, letters, paper airplanes, intimate pads. They whistled at visitors as they showed up, grading them from 1 to 10 and applauded emotional reunions. Some of the girls who had visitors would shout back at them *Why don't you go wash your asses, you shit-faces?*, while others chimed in, showing off their boyfriends, their brothers, and friends like trophies for them to choose from. Lala's appearance provoked whistles and applauses. Some gave her an 8, but the majority a 7, but there were a few 6s and someone yelled out a 9 in a husky, deep voice, like she had a cold. The same girl sailed a paper airplane from the fourth floor that landed two meters from Lala. It said, "I like you, sweetheart," framed by a heart. They mistook her for a man, every one of them.

She discovered three boys staring at her at the last train stop. One said she was a woman, the other two that she was a man. Before getting off, the one who was right couldn't contain his curiosity and pretending to be dumb, he went over and asked her.

"What's your name?"

"Lolo," Lala said, who, after all was said and done, hadn't lost her sense of humor.

"You can grab a table and two chairs," the guard in charge of visiting hours said, pointing to a corner of the yard.

He had just yelled up to the girls behind bars to cut it out if they wanted to go out on the roof that evening to see the eclipse. The effect was instantaneous, except for a couple of rebels who were silenced by their own companions. Lala went over to the plastic tables and chairs piled up in a corner. A girl was breast-feeding her baby at one of the tables while an older couple, probably her parents, watched her in silence. Lala dragged two chairs over to another corner in the yard. She sat down on one, moved to the second one, crossing and uncrossing her legs. She put the chairs back in place and stood quietly looking at the door and waiting . . .

12

Guayi came up to Lala from behind. Her hair was short and she was wearing a pair of men's pants and a tee-shirt of Los Ramones.

"There's your lover," the redhead told her, pointing to Lala at the other end of the yard.

Guayi stood there staring at the shaved back of her head and her dwarf ears. She saw herself sitting on top of Lala, pressing her hands down on the mattress. She was telling her to hold still. And Lala held still. She let Guayi grab her ears and pull them forward, turning her into a mouse. "You have the prettiest ears in the world. You've got to shave your head."

Guayi remembered all of this the second it took me to raise my snout from the corner where I had just peed. My legs propelled themselves forward. . . . I ran toward her barking. . . . I jumped up and down around her, nipped at her tee-shirt, smelled her ass, made her kneel down so I could cover her face with kisses. . . . It's great to be a dog! You can scream with happiness whenever you want to! Guayi put her arms around my neck and let me lick her all over the face.

"Hi, there, Chocolate Turd . . ."

It really turned me on when she called me that!

Bark.

"Yes, I missed you too . . ."

Bark! Bark!

"I know, I know."

We always understood each other fine. I would have stayed there, because I was just beginning to kiss her, but Guayi shoved my snout away so she could take a look at Lala. I stepped back without moving my butt.

"So, you did it . . . ," Guayi said, looking at her shaved head.

"Even my eyebrows."

I would have expected kisses, tears, hugs. But no, they didn't even touch each other.

"You have a strange head . . ."

Lala lifted her hand to her head, as though she wished to hide its oval shape. "Egghead," I heard one of the guys on the train say to the others.

"You came home . . ."

"No," Lala said. "Our house is back there. It'll be ready when we return."

"When we return?"

Something jarred Lala. It wasn't the question. It was the tone. She remembered all of Guayi's gestures, each inflexion of her voice. And this one was new. If there was something until now that Guayi hadn't shown, it was cynicism.

"I've come for you."

Guayi began to smile and ended up biting her lips. She always did that when she was too furious to get mad. She would peel the skin away with her teeth and end up with her lips raw.

"I should have been here," Lala said.

"Stop being an ass. We aren't going to talk about what could have been. If you came for me, you can just go on back. I'm not leaving here."

She walked across the yard and stopped in front of two girls playing cards on the only bench that was clean.

"Scram."

The two girls scrammed without a peep. Guayi sat down and gestured to Lala, slapping the bench.

"Come here," she said. "Sit down here."

Lala walked over and sat down beside her.

"I didn't know you were here. I swear I didn't know, which is why I didn't come before. I was waiting for you back there. When the package arrived, I thought you wouldn't be long. But the days passed and you didn't show. . . . Why didn't you tell them that I did it?"

"I didn't know where you were. When they came for me, I knew nothing about you . . ."

"Where did they find you?"

"At my cousin's. Two days after we left your house."

Lala looked down at the cement. Each square had a crack in it.

"But how?" she asked Guayi.

"Thanks to that jerk Mari . . . You remember Mari?"

"The Bolivian . . . ? The one who worked across the street . . ."

Guayi nodded.

"Her employers knew we were friends. They pressured her and she became scared. She's here without papers and was afraid they'd send her home. She gave the police the address. That very day they came for me."

"I don't understand . . . ," Lala said. "You sent the package a month ago . . ."

"It wasn't me who sent it, but my cousin. The money remained in his house, hidden in the videos. I thought he wouldn't send it. That he'd make off with it . . . But I had nothing to lose by taking a chance. If he'd found it, he would have kept it for himself."

"He didn't send all of it."

"I know. He told me he kept a thousand."

"More like five thousand."

Guayi smiled. The explanation didn't surprise her.

"In any case, he sent some. Come on, let's go for a walk."

She began to trace the perimeter of the fenced yard.

"Tell me how the house is going. It still didn't have a roof in the last letter my grandfather sent . . ."

I told you from the start. Lala does not cry in public. But if she'd opened her mouth at that moment . . . She clenched her throat and her jaw.

"Did you put in picture windows?"

That's why she let her talk, even if what Guayi was saying made no sense. She bit her lips and let her talk.

"My grandfather says it's the nicest lot of all. . . . We'll have to paint it some color so the boats can see it . . . Blue, okay? Do you like blue?"

There was one cement block in the entire yard that didn't have a crack in it. Lala stood on that block.

"I'm going to tell them it was me," she said. "I talked to my aunt. I'll talk to whoever I have to . . ."

Lala dried a couple of tears with the palm of her hand.

"I'm going to get you out of here . . ."

"Stop crying."

"I'm going to get you out of here," Lala said again, crying.

"We should have left earlier . . ."

It was what she repeated over and over every night, like a mantra that tortured her until dawn. She took four steps until she was standing in front of Lala. Four steps and suddenly the anger appeared. Everything had changed by the time she opened her mouth. Her face, the tension in her muscles, even the tone of her voice.

"How? Just what are you going to do to get me out of here? What are you going to tell them? That you killed him? Do you really believe your aunt is going to allow one of her nieces to end up in a place like this?"

She grabbed her by the arm and took her over to a corner.

"Stop crying," she repeated.

"Yes . . ."

"Stop . . ."

Lala closed her eyes hard, but she couldn't stop. She had to sit down on the ground. She no longer felt her bones when she cried like that. She hiccupped as she cried, making noises, with her nose running. They were watching her. The redhead walked over to them.

"Is everything all right?"

"Yes," Guayi said.

But the redhead didn't budge. She wasn't asking her.

"Yes," Lala said in a strangled voice.

"Start making your goodbyes. Visiting hours end in ten minutes."

She turned away and went over to the couple making out.

"Stand up," Guayi said.

Lala had no intention of getting up or stopping crying.

"Stand up."

They were going to have to drag her out of there.

"Do you really believe anyone's going to think you're capable of killing someone? Looking like that?"

Guayi squatted down beside her. Her chin was trembling, but Lala didn't see it.

"I can't even understand how you managed it . . . ," she said in a low voice. There was even a touch of scorn in her voice. "Just look at yourself . . ."

People around them were starting to say goodbye.

"Look at me."

Lala looked up.

"Do you want to help me?"

She nodded.

"Then leave. It's okay for me to be here. This is my place."

"You didn't do anything."

Guayi looked at her in silence, without saying a word more. They were so close that she could feel Lala's breath on her mouth.

"Go back or stay. Do what you want, but forget me. If you make a peep you're just going to create problems for me. Just when things here started to get better . . ."

"How can they get better?"

"Just believe me. There are things you can't understand."

She started to stand up, but Lala yanked her back by her tee-shirt.

"Why are you talking to me this way?"

Guayi ran her hand over the shaved head. A rapid caress that started in front and ended at the back of her neck. She grabbed Lala by the wrist with her other hand. She squeezed hard. Lala opened her fingers and let go of the tee-shirt.

The redhead opened the door in back and the other guard the door in front. (The visitors left by the door in front and the girls by the door in back, just like in life.)

"Anything else?" Guayi said shaking the dirt from her hands. "Even if I could get out of here, I wouldn't go back to you . . ."

"You're lying."

"Why'd you think I took the money? Why'd I leave without you?"

She said it without looking at her and it was worse than getting punched in the stomach.

"Because I wasn't going to go . . . I wasn't going anywhere if they hadn't caught me."

She got up and walked toward the door in back.

"Wait."

Guayi didn't turn around. She patted the shoulder of the girl in the pink jogging suit.

"Don't leave."

She grabbed her by the hair to turn her around.

"If you didn't want to have anything to do with me, why'd you send me the money?"

The guard ordered them inside, while the redhead grabbed Lala from behind.

"I didn't send it to you . . . ," Guayi said before disappearing. "I sent it to my grandfather."

She looked at her steady. She was telling the truth.

"Leave, Lala. Don't come back."

13

"Charo? Can you hear me?"

She cupped her hand around the mouthpiece and shouted again.

"Can you hear me?"

She was standing at a public phone on a street somewhere in La Plata. She had walked for hours, lost, until night fell and she ran right into the observatory. The corner was bustling with people, cars, people selling things, school buses. The first lunar eclipse of the century was that night. For some reason, people thought that was important.

"Yes, I visited her . . . Well, she's fine . . . Don't worry . . . We'll be home soon . . . How's the house going? Did they finish the roof?"

Her words got mixed up with those of the person next to her, who was shouting useless information in the phone. He was trying to convince the person on the other end of the line to get out of bed.

". . . It's not the same thing seeing it in person as seeing it on television. . . . It just isn't, because you've got four telescopes here, a reflecting mirror that is fifteen centimeters in diameter, a refraction lens with an opening of ten centimeters . . ."

A school bus pulled over in front of them. The doors opened, spitting out some twenty excited children. The teachers had them cross the street holding hands. Two of the boys were bending behind his back the arm of a fat, little, shortsighted kid yelling for help. No one heard him in the middle of the chaos of motors and voices.

"Yes, I promise I'll call again, soon. . . . No, I don't need money. I don't need a thing . . . Can I ask you to do me a favor? Paint it blue . . . The house, Charo, paint it blue . . . dark blue. . . . Yes, I swear to you that your granddaughter is fine. . . . My time is running out . . . I don't have any more coins . . . I will call again s . . ."

Across the street a man who worked for the observatory was distributing tickets to the kids to get in, while talking nonstop.

". . . During forty-seven minutes the moon will be completely hidden by the earth's surface . . ."

Lala crossed the street. She stuck out her hand to get a ticket.

"That'll be three pesos," the man said.

"I'm with them . . ."

The man looked at her dubiously. One of the boys, without losing his grip on the fat kid, interjected.

"She's the teacher's aide."

The man gave Lala a ticket and went on with his monologue.

"Do you understand what I'm saying? The moon will be totally hidden by the shadow of the earth and that's why the light will not reach it . . ."

"I always do the same thing when I ride the bus. Even if I have money," the smart-aleck one said to Lala. "Come on, let's go to the head of the line."

The rest of the kids followed them, all talking at the same time and not listening to each other.

"Are you coming to see the eclipse?"

"No."

"We aren't either."

The fat kid walked between the two of them with panic on his face.

"We're here because tonight he's going to make out with that girl over there," the smart-aleck said, pointing first to the fat boy and to a fat girl, all upset, who pulled up the rear and was paying attention to the teacher.

"Do you like her?"

"Yes," Lala said.

"Me too. If she weren't fat I'd make out with her myself. But fat people have to kiss other fat people, which is why he's going to be the one to make out with her."

"Does he want to?"

Lala looked at the fat kid.

"Do you want to?"

The fat kid nodded his head up and down rapidly. The bully hit him in the base of his head.

"Don't lie."

"He doesn't want to because he's queer," the other explained to her. But we're going to take care of it . . . Right, Tweety?"

The bully moved the kid's head up and down. The other kid didn't find the joke funny. He had just discovered that underneath her leather jacket Lala had tits.

"What's your name?" he asked her uneasily,

"Lala."

That startled the three guys.

"You're a woman?" Tweety said.

"Yes."

"You look like a man."

"I know."

There were about thirty persons on the terrace. They clustered in small groups around the telescopes and the refraction lens.

". . . What you are seeing here, on the southern edge of the moon, are the stars Castor and Pollux on the verge of being eclipsed in exactly . . . ," the man looked at the chronometer hanging from his neck, " . . . nine seconds."

There was a general commotion, as if something were about to change with the eclipse of some old stars like Castor and Pollux.

". . . 8, 7, 6, 5 . . ."

Lala saw how the bullies took advantage of the distraction to drag the fat boy off to the corner of the stairs.

". . . 4, 3, 2 . . ."

The fat, shortsighted kid was struggling, but without much conviction. The fat girl, who deep down was a romantic, knew it was best to do what they wanted, and fast, so as not to miss the eclipse.

"1 . . ."

Lala stepped back and saw how the fat girl was kissing the fat boy, grabbing him by the cheeks, as though she were kissing a doll.

"Give her a French kiss . . . ," the bully told him.

Lala had to grab onto the railing with both hands to remain

where she was. The only time they had messed with her was on a similar set of stairs. A shove, a split lip, and three missing teeth were enough for her not to be bothered again. She was never invited again to anyone's birthday party, but that didn't bother her. What was important was they never messed with her again.

"Zero!"

The stars disappeared.

People applauded.

"An eclipse within the eclipse," the guide shouted, with the enthusiasm of a magician.

The fat girl ran from the stairs and went over to the part of terrace where there was the least amount of people, right next to Lala.

"Move," she said to me.

I looked at Lala to see if I had to. She nodded. I moved my butt half a meter and watched the fat girl take a collapsible telescope out of her backpack. She had it all ready in a minute, with the precision of a sharpshooter.

"What you are seeing now is the lunar disk completely submerged in the umbra, the dark shadow of the earth . . . ," the guide was still saying. "The moon is seen with that coppery tone due to the refraction and the absorption of the sunlight in the earth's atmosphere . . ."

It wasn't a coppery tone. The moon was dyed a furious orange. Everything was colored differently, the sky, people's skin . . . Lala looked at her hands and then looked at me.

"You're colored purple," she said to me, smiling.

Her teeth were phosphorescent. The fat girl was smiling as she looked through her telescope. She looked up, full of emotion.

"It's the first total eclipse I've seen in my life," she whispered.

She offered Lala her telescope.

"Would you like to take a look?"

Lala didn't answer. Nothing upset her more than a friendly gesture.

"Go on, take a look . . ."

The fat girl put the telescope in her hands and helped her adjust the lens, holding the telescope with one hand and her head with the other.

"What you're seeing there are the moon's craters . . . ," she said pointing to the sky as if she had a telescope in her eyes.

And that's what Lala was seeing: she saw how the mountains and valleys were turning dark as the shadow of the earth crept over them.

"Can I ask you a question?"

Lala pulled her gaze away from the telescope and saw that the face of the fat girl was losing the copper tone it'd had for the last half hour.

"Would you like to live up there?" the fat girl asked her. "All alone?"

She didn't wait for Lala to answer.

"I sure would," she said.

And she seemed to feel better just by having said it.

"Look . . . Don't miss the ending."

Lala looked through the telescope again. The colors were changing.

"Right now the moon is emerging from the shadow of the earth . . . ," the guide was saying gravely. Do you see it? It is

beginning to shine by the full light of the sun. The total phase
has ended . . ."

Lala stopped listening to him. She wasn't interested in scien-
tific explanations. It was natural, from that day on, for the colors
of the earth to change.

14

The day dawned full of dampness. We saw the clouds roll in
as it got lighter from where we were in a service station a block
from the Institute. Lala bought a cup of coffee and a small bottle
of rum with her last money. She thought she'd make it last, but
she downed it in one gulp while still thinking about it. She
wanted to get warm. She felt like she was frozen and it wasn't
because of the weather. She spent the rest of the night staring at
the windows of the Institute. She washed her face at seven in the
station's bathroom and five minutes later she was at the door. She
was met by the redhead guard. "Visiting hours start in an hour,"
she told her. She'd have to wait. The guard waited until eight,
when Lala went up to her again, to tell her that Guayi was sick
and she wouldn't be able to see her that day.

"Why not?"

"Because she doesn't want to."

"Let her tell me."

"She told you yesterday. I'm telling you today. And tomorrow
as well."

She didn't have enough money for the train back. We dodged
the guard by moving from one car to another, but they caught up
with us at Constitution. Nothing happened to Lala. They let her

go when they realized she had nothing of value. She didn't stop to consider where she'd go, but just let her body carry her along. And it brought her here, to the domain of the trainer, who stared at her without going over from the other side of the fence as he tightened the blood-stained bandage of his only employee.

"What are you going to do with the dog?" the kid asked him, holding his wounded hand and pale from the amount of pain he'd withstood.

"The dog's not to blame. You had the cuff on wrong. Go on. You have to take the antirabies injection. Take the rest of the day off."

The kid went off with his tail between his legs without arguing. The one who was barking its head of was the Sheepdog that had attacked him in the middle of the training. It was the only dog barking. The others were watching the whole thing from their cages. Two or three were loose, but didn't bother to come over. The most restless one was going in a circle chasing its own tail. They all knew that, in the land of the trainer, barking'll get you thrown out.

"It's you, right?"

"I guess so," Lala said.

He saw me sitting about a meter behind her.

"Yes, it's you."

He wiped the blood from the leg of his pants and walked over to the fence. Lala looked at the blood while the trainer looked at her tits.

"What happened?"

"A work-related accident. Poor kid. He's useless. I'm going to have to fire him."

He spoke in telegraphic sentences with a monotonous tone, little used to the subtleties of the human world.

"As far as training is concerned?"

"I'm here to do the training. He's useless as a bit player."

"What's that mean?"

"Someone who pretends he's the thief."

A burst of thunder crowned his sentence at the period, just as in a bad movie.

"Fuck him. I'm going to have to find someone else," he said as he folded the aluminum cuffs the kid had put on wrong.

"What's the job entail?"

"Teaching the dog to bite and attack."

"I can do that."

"You?"

He let a smile slip. He could have been a leading man in the movies, but he slurred his words and his mouth was a mess, his lips split and two teeth missing.

"I need a job."

There was a strange silence, of the kind that ends quickly. The sky was about to break open at any minute. It was so heavy that from where I stood Lala's head was wrapped in clouds.

"Come on in."

The trainer didn't move. Two of his dogs met Lala at the door, as though they were part of her body.

"Let's go inside before it starts to rain."

His house was in back of the lot. More than a house it was a hut, but assembled with great effort. Taken separately, each piece of furniture there, picked up from the garbage cans of the North End, was hideous. But taken together, the hideous pieces made up a harmonious whole, a mysteriously harmonic whole, as though each piece made the one next to it look attractive. The trainer reached over for the teakettle. He knew where each item was with millimetric precision.

"Come in."

The two dogs stayed outside the door. They let me go in because they had no choice, knowing that the trainer was keeping an eye on them. Lala stood in the doorway, watching him fold the two aluminum cuffs.

"And what makes you think you can do something like that?"

"Because I understand dogs," Lala said. "I'm not afraid of them. I like them."

She did not answer standing in the doorway. She said the first sentence as she walked in and the second as she put on one of the aluminum cuffs, and the third as she removed the trainer's wallet from his pocket as he said, "That's not enough."

The dogs saw how Lala's hand went in and out of his pocket at the same time as the trainer turned to face the door and ask her what the hell she was doing. The upset tone of his voice was enough. The two dogs chased Lala as she adjusted the second cuff in the rain. She thrust her bended arm in the mouth of the first dog, cutting off his barking. She caught the second dog in the air with the assuredness of someone who has spent her life wearing aluminum cuffs. The dog fell on its back and renewed the attack. But a whistle stopped him. The trainer held Lala's gaze. She still had one of the dogs hanging from the cuff, his teeth sunk in as though his life depended on it.

Lala contemplated her naked body in the piece of mirror. Her eyes were more yellow than ever, and the pockets underlining them made them look like cat's eyes. She didn't care if they were yellow or brown. That's why what she had just done had turned out good for her, because that day she really didn't care. It didn't matter if she lost her arm or landed a job.

"You can stay here."

"And you?"

She had put on the sweater the trainer had given her. His voice reached her from the other side of the curtain separating the room from the rest of the hut.

"I'm not living here. . . . And my guess is that if you don't have a dry sweater to put on you don't have a bed to sleep in."

It was a strange reasoning. But correct in this case.

"With or without sugar?"

"I don't care."

She hated people who didn't care. But now, for the first time, her own apathy made her feel comfortable. The water was about to boil when she pulled the curtain back again. The trainer put a couple of spoonfuls of coffee in the maté gourd and gave it first to Lala, without sugar.

"Here. This'll make you feel better."

Lala felt how the hot liquid ran through her body. Her arms and legs were numb.

"I thought I wouldn't see you again."

"Me neither."

"The one who showed up again was your brother. It looks like

they're about to release him. Every so often they let him out for
the afternoon. The treatment doesn't do them much good. Every
time they let someone go he comes right over here. He asked me
about you the last time I saw him."

He paused. Lala didn't ask a thing.

"Don't you want to know how he's doing?"

"No."

She finished folding the aluminum cuffs without saying a
thing.

"Okay. Let's not talk about you. Let's talk about me."

He waited for some response. But all Lala did was hand him
the maté gourd and finish hanging her wet clothes on the only
chair, over by the stove. She was also surprised by what was happening to her. Until the day before, they had given her an anesthetic only once in her life, when they removed her appendix.
When she came out of the anesthetic she felt like her life was
slipping out her bellybutton. Guayi had fallen asleep in the chair
with her head rocking back and forth and her hand resting on
Lala's stomach. But she opened her eyes when she felt every last
one of the muscles tense up.

"What are you doing here?" Lala asked. She was already
dreaming about Guayi but was afraid to tell her.

"Your mother asked me to stay here until your aunt came. She
had an appointment at the beauty shop and your father had a
speech to give."

Lala raised her arm and she could see the whole thing in a
single arc, a gelatinous blob.

"What's wrong with you?"

"I don't know."

And there was Guayi jumping from one side of the bed to the other.

"You're all over the place . . ."

"It is the anesthesia."

"No, it isn't."

Guayi got up from the chair and stood at the end of the bed.

"I'm going to call the nurse . . . ," she said dragging her feet.

"Don't call anyone. Don't let go of me."

Lala fixed onto Guayi's eyes and they stayed like that . . . Guayi pulling on her feet as though they were the string of a balloon drifting through the air.

"Aren't you going to ask me who I'm living with?" the trainer asked her.

Lala raised her head and made an effort to understand him. The day before, in the yard of the Institute, Guayi had let her go. Ever since then she had felt the anesthesia. The world was drifting away and the only thing she had within reach, right before her, was the void.

"I think you met him . . ."

"You live with a man?"

"No. The client's dog I live with. I was training him the night we met. Just got here from the United States."

"The dog?"

"No, my client. The dog, too. She had gotten him over there. She'd paid a thousand dollars for him and was afraid he'd be stolen. 'Make him mean,' she told me, 'as mean as you can.' She lived alone. She told me her husband had stayed on working in the States. Then I found out from another client that he was in jail . . ."

I was the only one listening to him. The world had gone mute for Lala and the only words floating in the air were Guayi's.

"I think he hid a job that turned out bad. They gave him five years. He has four left. She said he's in one of those fancy jails, the ones for people with money. They've got everything. Cable, heat, special meals. Who knows if it's true, but that's what she said. When I finished training the dog I was already living with her. . . . You know what she calls me? My Little Prince. One day I told her I liked those little Kinder eggs and now every night she puts one on my pillow. She even made a shelf for the toys they have inside."

The lights of a car shone through the windows and lighted up the house, followed by four dry short blasts of the horn. The trainer didn't even have to look to see who it was.

"There she is. She comes for me every day after she goes to the gym. The two maids are waiting for us at home with dinner and the bath ready. I come from a family of nine children. Get the picture?"

Of course I did. There's nothing nicer than being a lap dog.

"Do you love her?" I thought, although it's what Lala said.

"She loves me."

It was raining like mad outside. The trainer zipped up the jacket his client had given him.

"Can I ask you for something else? Stay here. I don't want her to see you . . . ," he begged Lala, running his hand over her head. "It looks like shit."

He quickly kissed her on the mouth.

"You smell just like the first time."

"You can't remember that."

"I remember everything that happened that night . . ."

Lala looked out the window and saw the trainer running over toward the imported car waiting for him by the entrance to the lot. When he opened the door, she got a glimpse of the snout of a Chinese dog and a platinum-blond head. She imagined him sitting on the leopard-skin upholstery, going to a three-storey house to find dinner and the Jacuzzi ready. He was the only man she'd ever kissed in her life. But what she recalled that night was not his kisses, but Guayi, watching them.

15

It's a lie. I'm the only one who remembers everything that happened on the final night of last year. Everyone else was either too
doped out or drunk to remember it. Felicitas called at seven to
invite them to a dinner she was putting together in her apartment.
Brontë told her he preferred to stay at home with the children. He
hung up and called Lala on the intercom. He told her to go buy a
turkey, angel hair spaghetti, nougat, cider, champagne, and all the
other crap his wife bought for the holidays. He asked her for a
bottle of whiskey and cigarettes. "Not a carton, one pack." He gave
her a couple of hundred-peso bills and sent her off. Brontë was
having a good night. There were few of them, but when he had
them he could captivate whoever came by. The end of the year
had made him nostalgic and he felt like something important was
about to happen. He went into Pep's room and rummaged in his
drawers until he found some marihuana and paper for rolling it.
He smoked some in his study while he wrote the epilogue to his
latest success and then smoked more when he stepped out of the
shower. The third whiskey got his courage up and he went ahead
with the razor, and five minutes later his face was smooth. When
he went down to the kitchen, Lala and Guayi were decorating the
turkey with the angel hair and he balanced himself in his sobriety
so as not to fall down the stairs.

Lala turned on the TV in the trainer's hut. The channel didn't matter. A forty-two-year-old German, a computer engineer, was addressing a jury. He was confessing as to how he killed, quartered, and ate the remains of a man he met on the Internet. His ad drew strong young men, between eighteen and thirty, to be devoured. "I wanted him to become part of my body. I remembered him in every piece of meat I ate. It was like communion," the German was saying. Lala didn't even blink. "During the act I felt hatred, rage, and joy at the same time. I had wanted that my whole life. When I was eight I had fantasies of eating my school mates." Lala stopped listening, although the man went on. He lived alone with his mother and felt himself abandoned, obsessed by the idea of having a brother, "someone outside of me." He ended up creating an imaginary one called Frank, he said, while Lala looked at his eyes. In mid-2000 he began to post ads on the Internet in search of a man to kill. He said, "there are hundreds of persons attempting to satisfy their desire of either eating human flesh or being devoured." Lala changed the channel and tried to dismiss her recollections, but Brontë had come back to life.

"I'd like to stop fucking around with essays and sit down and write fiction," he said to Lala and Guayi. "In the end, fiction is all that matters."

Pep was levitating when he came down to dinner. He had smoked a whole one of the stuff imported from Holland and the effect had been the opposite. It had plunged him into himself, while Brontë was possessed by a florid and branching flood of words. When Guayi brought the turkey in, he took the knife from her hands.

"I'll serve today," he said. "There's a place setting missing."

Guayi checked the table.

"They're three settings. No one's missing."

"You're missing. Go on. Get a plate for yourself."

"That's not necessary."

"It's New Year's and you're part of the family. You can't stay in the kitchen by yourself."

"Really, it's not . . ."

"I'll decide what's necessary. Go on."

Guayi came and went from the kitchen with plates, silverware, and glasses, while Brontë whistled as he carved the turkey.

"Leg or breast?"

"Leg," Lala said.

"Leg," Pep said.

"One of you is going to have to eat breast because I like the leg . . ."

He looked at his two children, and in a Solomonic rapture, he served himself the two legs.

"It's better for the two of you to eat breast so you won't fight. Sit down over there . . . ," he said to Guayi, pointing to Sasha's place with the tip of the knife. "Great. Now we're all here. Eat up."

And he began, without realizing that he was the only one who had food on his plate.

"What would you like?" Lala asked Guayi.

"Whatever."

"I can't give you whatever. A leg's not the same as a breast. You choose."

Guayi didn't know what to say, as she looked at the serving platter. Lala randomly speared something for her, but Brontë stopped her in midair with the tip of the knife.

"No. Have her decide. It's all the same to you? Was it all the same to you to stay in Paraguay or come here?"

"No."

"Huh?"

"No."

"See? It isn't all the same. What do you want? I mean, from life, what do you want?"

"Leave her alone."

"Don't go getting jealous on me. . . . What do you want? Do you want to clean my house for the rest of your life?"

"Why are you talking to her like that? It's all the same to you, too."

"For her to clean?"

"Your life."

Brontë smiled. It was the first night that month he didn't feel like committing suicide.

"No. I'm at peace because I have you. When I get old, when it's all the same to me, you'll help me. . . . You'll be the protagonist," he said to Lala, without thinking about what he was saying, turning to look at Guayi. "Would you like to tell me the story of your life?"

Guayi lowered her eyes. She was used to others looking at her like that, but never someone like Brontë, who was in the newspaper and on television. And it wasn't because he was famous. Guayi clearly understood that fame and prestige were not the same thing. And Brontë possessed that: prestige and culture. He had a study full of books and he had read them all.

"I once had the chance to be an actress," she said.

It was the first time she had said anything about herself in four years.

"But I said no. I don't like cameras, but books . . ."

She respected them. You could tell just by the way in which she dusted the television and the books. She had a different soft touch for the covers. Guayi didn't forget about the bookcase the night they designed the house. She wanted one like Brontë's, floor to ceiling, built into the wall.

"I didn't ask you what you'd been offered. . . . I asked you what you want."

"To sing."

"You want to be a singer?"

"I want to sing in Guaraní."

"Only in Guaraní?"

"I can't sing if it's not in Guaraní."

"Let's see . . . Sing something to me."

"That's enough," Lala said, trying to get rid of the echo of Brontë's words and saying to Guayi, "No singing."

"But she's dying to . . . Aren't you dying to?"

Guayi turned red. Never, in all the time since her arrival in Buenos Aires, had she been so servile toward him. His attention had calmed her more than his orders. She wiped her mouth with the napkin and breathed deep as though to clear her lungs. At first it was no more than a murmur and Brontë had to sit up to hear her. Her voice sounded different, deep, velvety, Indian, and came from the pit of her stomach. As it filled the space it became thicker, like all the birds were singing together. It didn't last long, barely a minute. Brontë smiled in silence, raising a forkful of food to his mouth.

"Guaraní is lovely sounding. You'll have to sing more often," he said to Guayi with his mouth full. "Do you see what a great cook this girl is, how she sings, and what a face on her?" he said to Lala all in one question, as if it were all the same. "Listen to what I'm saying. . . . She doesn't realize it," he said chuckling. "It's doing you good to be in this house. You're getting prettier by the day."

He swallowed the food with sip of wine and took advantage of the pause to take a deep breath before going on.

"Would you like to be the main character in a book?"

"Leave her alone," Lala said.

"Would you like it?"

Guayi smiled and lowered her eyes. It was a sign of victory for Brontë.

"Then it's a deal," Brontë said, touching his glass to Guayi's, which remained empty. "Let's write a small story. Not too important . . . Like an afternoon . . . Like my life . . . As Mao Tse-tung says, 'An army without culture, is an ignorant army, and an ignorant army cannot defeat the enemy. . . . ' Do you know what that means?"

Guayi shook her head no. She might as well have said yes. Brontë forged ahead.

"It means that the job of the workers in art and literature is to merge with the proletariat and create literature and art in their service . . ."

"I've got to go," Pep interrupted him. Pep had an infallible radar for knowing when to eject himself from a situation. "They're waiting for me at the hospital . . ."

He had eaten without looking up from his plate. He was under scrutiny ever since they had found the plants. They called it probation. Brontë had to pull some strings to keep him out of jail. He finally managed a temporary suspended sentence. Pep tore out the plant trailings, admitted his responsibility to the judge (a childhood friend of Brontë), and accepted in silence the year of psychological treatment and voluntary social service in the hospital in San Isidro.

"Open the champagne before you leave," Brontë said. "Let's toast. Then everyone can do whatever he wants."

He smiled as he watched his son uncork the champagne. Pep had presented him with the best media campaign anyone could have invented. The day he was given probation, they came to interview him for a series of documentaries on Argentine writers. When they asked about his children, Brontë talked about the only thing that came to mind, how he had saved his son from jail. He rattled the wasp's nest just for a little bit of fun. He showed them the garden and told them that two of those plants were his. He was tired of being a serious writer and wanted to change his image. And it worked. Those who read him continued to read him (in order to understand) and those who didn't read him tried him (they thought it was great to have a marihuana garden on your rooftop). After the documentary was shown, a day didn't go by without a young and nervous journalist coming by the house to write an article for some literature journal on the Internet. And the state of the house, along with the record of his failed suicide attempts, enhanced the mysticism. Brontë, who more than a good writer was a good businessman, sensed that his next book, which he had just completed that very night, should be called *Aimless, the Generation of 2000*. He served the wine as he looked at his children, anonymous protagonists of his next book.

"To the future!" he said to them.

He was no longer looking at them, but at Guayi.

"I'm going to dedicate it to you, okay? We could begin right today. I'm getting an idea for the beginning . . ."

He wasn't getting any ideas. Not even that three nights later she would come into his room and get in bed with him. His mind was a blank.

"What's for dessert?"

"I'll go get it," Guayi said.

She had to grab onto the marble counter in the kitchen because she was shaking with the thought about herself as a heroine.

"Don't get involved with him," Lala told her.

"What do you mean?"

Lala noticed how Brontë for the first time was gazing at Guayi. Brontë broke the tension by laughing gaily, like a muzzled wolf, patting his daughter on the cheek.

"You're right. Better to leave with her. You two have fun."

But Lala wasn't looking at him. She was looking at the painting by Alonso that framed him. And she was doing the math. She had just sold the furniture, but Guayi was more stubborn than ever. They still didn't have enough even to buy the plot of land on the lake. She went into the kitchen and put two bottles of champagne in her bag. Guayi was just finishing garnishing the dessert plates.

"Let's go."

"Now?"

"Yes, now."

"But we were going to . . ."

"Tomorrow he won't remember a thing."

Guayi didn't believe her. It was something else—jealousy—because he had never offered even to dedicate anything to her. But she didn't say that.

"Hurry. I need for you to help me. Pep won't wait for us."

They both knew he wasn't going to the hospital. He'd had to get rid of the plants, but not his vices. She intercepted him on the stairs, while Guayi changed and Brontë smoked a cigar and talked to Sasha's tree, which had died when they stopped watering it with Bach's Flowers.

"We're going with you."

It wasn't a question. There was a price to be paid for being the silent accomplice of her brother. They waited for Brontë to shut himself up in his study before taking down Alonso's painting.

"It's too big . . . He's going to notice."

"He doesn't look at the walls."

Lala's argument was that in that house no one looked at the paintings and it made no sense for them to be there. On the other hand, they could change their future. Guayi tried to find a reason why they shouldn't. She really wasn't worried that Brontë would get mad, but that he would change his opinion about her and she would end up without her book. But Lala ignored her and began to wrap the picture. Pep didn't ask any questions when he saw his sister putting the painting in the bed of the truck. He started the motor and gunned it as a sign that he was leaving.

"Are you going to leave him alone?"

"Yes."

She had seen him watching them from his study window. He was smiling. And for the first time, Guayi smiled back at him. Guayi liked anyone who would look at her with those eyes. Someone else's desire was her desire . . .

"I'm not going to any fancy party," Guayi said as they drove off to the hut where Pep conducted his business.

Los Chinos is not a typical slum. The vast majority of its inhabitants are children of the rich who exchanged their roots for the path of art, in hippyism and perdition. Painters, musicians, and artisans hung up their suits as future leaders of the world and squatted on a portion of river landfill. Others came later, people who had nothing and blended in. But Pep's friend was one of the founders. His hut was in the heart of Los Chinos.

"Me neither," Lala said.

She had no intention of staying there for any time at all. What she wanted fit in the palm of her hand. If ecstasy didn't come that night on its own, she would help it along with a pill.

"There's someone I want you to meet."

The hut was crammed with electronics. It was the husk of the third world filled with the first world. DVDs, CD burners, imported karaoke sets. Shelves full of records and a water bed, even a basketball hoop in the shape of a guillotine and a transparent ball with Osama bin Laden's head in the center. The roof of the hut had a Direct TV antenna and there was a flat screen hanging on the wall like a painting. He bought everything by Internet and had his clients bring it from Miami whenever they traveled there. He could have left the neighborhood a long time ago, but he felt secure there and had everything he needed.

"They might be fucking capitalists, but they're clever," Pep's friend was saying as we walked into the hut.

He dribbled the head three times before throwing it at the hoop. Bin Laden flew through the air and dropped through the guillotine. He was in a good mood that night. He'd never sold so much. Pepito was counting the thirty pills he'd ordered from him to cover the demand at the party. Another pickup was already waiting at the door.

"Here. Happy New Year," he said to Lala as he placed three pills in her hand. "For you, for your friend, and for my neighbor."

His neighbor was the trainer. We found him lying on his back in the grass, waiting for the fireworks. Lala ripped the wrapping paper off the painting and set it in front of his eyes.

"How much?"

The trainer saw Alonso's signature in the right-hand corner of the painting. An original. He looked up. Lala was smiling at him over the edge of the frame, looking like a happy decapitated head.

"Much more than the others you brought me."

"How long will it take?"

"I can't see him before the end of the week. It's up to him. But I guess a week."

He was talking about the client that unloaded the paintings
for him. The trainer worked with his two Dobermans twice a
week.

"Tell him I'm in a hurry."

The sky lighted up at midnight. We began to feel like our
bones and jaws were going soft. I include myself because Lala
hadn't forgotten me. She cut a small piece off her pill, put it on
my tongue and held my snout closed until I swallowed it. Spread
out on the grass, cradled between sky and earth, Guayi turned
her head in slow motion to look at Lala.

"What do you think the beginning is?"

"Of what?"

"Our novel."

"Your novel. He made you the offer."

"If it's about me, it's about you."

I didn't know what she was talking about. The words lost their
shape along with her body, which was dancing without rhythm
and as she had no bones on the shadow of the trainer. She followed him to the hut with the excuse that she wanted to see
what it looked like on the inside. The trainer leaned the painting
in a corner, away from the stove and the windows, and covered it
with a cloth, and when he turned around he found Guayi's
mouth was waiting for him. I shouldn't tell you this, because sup-
posedly I didn't see it. It took me a while to get up from the grass.
I turned with my legs all stretched out, covering myself with the
dew until I ran into Lala. She jumped when I bumped into her.
When she walked into the hut, she found them on the bed.
Guayi put out her hand and pulled her over. Lala let her lay her

down beside her and remove her dress. Guayi's hands around her waist gave way to the trainer's.

"Don't look at him. Look at me."

A news item pulled Lala away from her recollections. It hadn't been long since the trainer had left, leaving her alone. She was sitting in front of the television, watching the screen without seeing a thing. Until two faces she recognized came on. The bullies who had helped her get into the observatory the night before. They were school shots and they were smiling at the camera, standing in the schoolyard.

". . . The tragedy happened today in a private school in La Plata . . . ," the announcer was saying. "Martín Paz and Juan Lartirigoyen were killed by one of their classmates . . ."

The photographs of the two bullies overlapped with the one of the fat kid. The big cheeks of his smile swallowed his eyes.

"His friends called him Tweety. He was shy, but everyone liked him. He showed up at school today with his father's gun in his backpack. He shot both boys twice. When asked why he did it, he said, 'To teach them a lesson.' He wouldn't say anything else . . ."

Beneath the fat kid there was the superimposed legend "To teach them a lesson." His end-of-the-year school picture had become a mug shot.

16

The police station in Martínez looks like it could be used as a
film set. Starched uniforms, late-model patrol cars, freshly
painted walls, leafy trees in front of the main entrance . . . a
mirage of what Argentina could be. That day, instead of just
seeming to be, it was really a film set, for the filming of the final
episode of a soap opera that made reality (charges of robbery and
collisions, transfer of prisoners, statements . . .) turn into a back-
ground. And no one seemed to be bothered by it. Quite the con-
trary. People came and went like a tame flock of sheep when the
assistant director shouted "Cut!" Lala leaned against the side of a
motor home to watch the scene. There was a woman standing
next to her with her hands cuffed behind her back, escorted by
two officers. None of the onlookers looked at her, only the main
characters, who were kissing at the door of the station before
going their separate ways. Lala felt a blow on her spine. The
make-up girl was trying to open the door of the motor home.

"Move, sweetheart. Go stand over there. We've got work to
do," she said without saying she was sorry for banging her.

"Here I am ready to confess my guilt for murder," Lala
thought, making her way over to the door. Inside, the chaos was
more intense. A bit later I heard that it was the first or the last

time that police station had been used as a set. At the same time it was impossible to get help at any of the police stations in Buenos Aires and difficult in the suburbs, Police Captain Mastrangelo cooperated on only one condition. There had to be a part for him, and better yet if it involved a few lines of dialogue. Of course, he didn't say so in so many words. As you are about to see, Mastrangelo has class. The officer who took the call from each producer had been ordered to ask two questions and only two questions: what the scene was like and whether there was a role for the Captain. If the answer was in the affirmative, they turned to the details. If it was in the negative, the Captain had a conflict that day and any every day after. The producers had gotten the idea, and so now there was always a role for the Captain.

"I'm here to see Captain Mastrangelo," Lala said to the only officer waiting on the public.

He was made up. They put eyeliner on him and a base that was too dark for his skin. Lala thought at first he was an actor, but no, he was what he was, a policeman with makeup. He'd had his debut in the last scene.

"Who's asking for him?"

"Paula Brontë."

"He's busy."

"I'll wait."

"What's your business?"

"It's a private matter."

"What?"

"It's private."

Lala stepped aside for two electricians carrying lights into the captain's office and sat down to wait. There was barely room to move. Behind the counter the makeup girl was smoothing out the base on a corporal who was going to escort the main lead into the captain's office in the next scene.

"Move along. Come on, outside!" the made-up policeman requested of those who had no concrete reason to be there.

A crazed fat lady pressed herself against the counter.

"I have a crime to report," she lied.

"What about?"

"The . . . theft . . . uh . . . of . . . a wallet . . ."

"Are you aware that making false statements is a crime? Are you certain that's what you want to do?"

The fat lady doubted for half a second. Was she willing to give up her liberty to be, for half an hour, less than a meter away from the main actors? When she saw them go in her heart started racing so much it made her dizzy. The policeman ignored her and opened the captain's office door. A glow of artificial light was streaming out. Lala went over in her head what she was going to say. Yes, Guayi was in the house that night, but she was sleeping in her room. She did it by herself, with no accomplice. Seven ketamine tablets dissolved in a glass of milk. No, he'd never hit her. No, not that either. Just because. There are things that just happen. After the questions would come the psychiatric tests, the press . . . months of comings and goings before any decision was made. If she needed a year's salary in her job as a trainer to pay the fees of a decent lawyer, a little bit of press coverage and more than one would be willing to take the case for free. She only had a month to reopen Guayi's case and get her sentence dismissed. Lala just knew that after she was transferred to Ezeiza, things would be a lot more complicated.

"Heh . . . miss . . ."

She looked over at the door and saw the policeman emerging.

"Go on in."

He stepped aside to let her pass. Mastrangelo was seated behind his desk with his face turned up so the makeup girl could do a good job of masking the bags under his eyes. He had studied his pose and wanted Felicitas to see his side as an actor in all its splendor.

"Come in, Felicitas, come in . . ."

It was stuffy in there. The female lead was going over her lines with the script man, the director was giving instructions to the cameraman, the woman in charge of continuity was seducing the chief of production. The electricians were threading their way between everyone with their cables. Mastrangelo opened one of his eyes to catch a glimpse of her. And he opened them wide, making a mess of the mask and the eyeliner, when he saw that the Brontë asking for him was the niece and not the aunt.

"Can you give me ten minutes?" he asked the director.

"Five."

"Come on."

He grabbed Lala by the arm to lead her out of the office. He took her to the end of the hall and without knocking walked into the only office that was still working. The made-up policeman was taking a statement from the fat lady, who was making up the details of the robbery. Mastrangelo ordered them to continue their business elsewhere and the policeman was in no mood to contradict him. On the days when they're filming, the captain is like a powder keg. He picked up the typewriter and asked the fat

lady to follow him. Mastrangelo closed the door in such a hurry
that he left me standing outside.

"I'm happy to see you . . . ," I heard him say on the other side
of the door.

Silence.

"Your aunt told me that you were by the house for just one
night . . . that you disappeared again the next morning. She hasn't
heard a word from you in two months. She's very worried
and . . ."

"What has to be done to reopen the case?" Lala interrupted
him.

"What was that?"

"I want to reopen the case."

Silence.

I'm sorry, but I missed what came next. The made-up policeman saw me sniffing at the door and showed me out the front
door with a kick in my ass. All the uproar had left him in a bad
mood. Not the uproar as such, but because it made him sweat.
The sweat made his makeup run and all he wanted to do was to
go home and tell his wife he had acted in a soap opera and show
her that, with a little help, his face wasn't so ugly after all. Fifteen minutes later one of the technicians opened the door to go
out and smoke a cigarette and I snuck in quiet as a mouse
because one thing I learned in my life is that no one looks down.
The only one left in the office was Mastrangelo, dialing a number
with the receiver jammed between his shoulder and his head.

"Felicitas? Yes, it's me, Mastrangelo. Listen to me. She's here.
Your niece . . . Calm down. I know what has to be done . . . Just

what you told me she'd say. Poor thing. No, she's not going to leave . . . Because not . . . Because they're taking her statement . . ."

And then out of the blue.

"What if she's telling the truth?"

He clutched the receiver as though a hurricane were passing through his ear.

"No, I'm not yanking you around . . . Okay, take it easy. She's fine, just fine. . . . You're right. It's more than likely that . . ."

He liked Felicitas enough not to make a mess of things. Especially, given that it was one of the few cases that had been solved so neatly that he had framed on the walls of his office news clippings from various sources in the press praising the work of his division. Just at that moment the assistant director stuck his head through the half-opened door.

"We're ready, Miki."

"Be right there."

The assistant walked down the hall, yelling for everyone to be quiet, with the sort of authority Mastrangelo could never muster.

"I've got to go. Okay. Come over. But if they come with the ambulance, tell them to park it on the corner. It's a madhouse over here."

When the director yelled "Action!" Lala was about to begin the farce. Seated in front of her, the made-up policeman, who no longer even had a desk, was getting ready to take her statement, the typewriter resting on his legs. Mastrangelo had sent them out in back of the station, close to where the holding cells were. His orders were clear. "It doesn't matter what she says. You just type. If she stops, just ask her anything. But don't let her leave." He began to sweat again, paralyzed by the pressure of combining typing with acting. Lala saw him put a sheet of paper without official letterhead in the typewriter.

"You're going to type on that kind of paper?"

The guy nodded. It was an insignificant detail but at the same time a crucial one. Lala knew that whatever she said would end up crumpled in some wastebasket. How could it be so difficult to prove that you're guilty? To make a clean confession, turn yourself in, ask for justice to be done? Even the prisoners. She asked to go to the bathroom for a minute, walked past the door without stopping and signaled for me to follow her. Someone asked her for an autograph when she emerged, convinced that a bald woman without eyebrows must be famous. Lala gave her one.

17

We found the trainer kneeling on the grass, showing a Poodle how to stand on two legs. His sister was watching her with her head turned to the left. What he was doing made no sense. They were Thalía and Shakira, two animals who, in addition to being filthy, were having serious learning problems. But the trainer never lost his cool. It didn't matter if his student was slow or simply an imbecile. He believed in them implicitly. And he got good results. Even those who hadn't been born to bowl you over left the school with one or two tricks under their arm. But that day he was glum and silent and in a bad mood. Lala thought it was her fault. She had asked him for an hour off for lunch and had been gone for two. They had been working together for two weeks again, seventeen days, to be exact. And her efforts were a long way from what she promised.

Last Monday she didn't even wake up at the school. She spent Guayi's birthday at the door of the Institute, in front of one of the windows that looked out on the fourth floor. If she didn't want to see her, at least she was going to know that she was there. She took her a cake that was crooked and had gone flat (the first she ever made in her life) and she asked the redhead guard to get it to her. It was days like today that Lala thought she was in jail and Guayi was abusing her liberty. The trainer told her on Tuesday that it was the last time she was going to disappear like that. If she blew it again she'd be out of a job. Lala was certain that day had arrived when she came back late from the police station. She put on the aluminum sleeves without looking him in the face and they worked in silence until the end of the afternoon. The routine was always the same. The dogs arrived at six, basic training until noon, lunch, advanced training until five, baths, and then deliver the dogs. Basic training is to civilize them, while advanced training is to turn them into killing machines. Lala spent the day offering up her body every time the trainer gave the signal to attack. Her arms hurt so much when it started to get dark that she had to massage them to stop them from shaking. But she did it out of sight. They delivered the last dogs at seven-thirty. They put three Labradors in a pickup full of kids and the two Poodles in a hired car that came for them every afternoon. Lala saw Socrates's smile looking out from under the open shirt of the driver. Deformed by the pressure on the material from his gut, he looked more like one of the Stooges.

"Something's going to happen," she thought.

Guayi had taught her to believe in that. It means something's going to happen when the past comes back. Socrates was not the only one. The day before she had seen Pep in Los Chinos. She saw his pickup driving through the dirty streets of the neighborhood while she was baking Guayi's cake. She dropped what she was doing and followed him. Pep parked his pickup at the door of his friend's hut. His hair hadn't grown very much since the last time he'd pulled up the trailings. He had his head shaved like Lala. The same color, the same shape of the head. In fact, they looked more alike than ever. Lala didn't even notice, tossing her clothes on mindlessly and without looking in the mirror. But they were even dressed alike, in worn pants and white tee-shirts. Lala went to meet him when he emerged from the hut and they stood face-to-face for a moment. She walked off and he climbed into the pickup. He sat there with the key in his hand, watching her walk away through the rearview mirror. Could it be that . . . ? Of course not. He started the motor and pulled away. Some time back his brain had begun to play tricks on him and he lived with these hallucinations. The truck sped by us without stopping.

"Are you going to tell me what's going on?"

"Why do you think something's going on?"

"Because I know you. You're on the point of saying something and you don't know whether to tell me or not."

"I'll tell you tomorrow."

"No. Today."

"There's not enough time today."

"You're going to fire me."

Silence. I came out of the room and sat down beneath Lala's feet. This wasn't any time to ruin my image. The trainer was smoking, staring out the window. His client must have been coming by any moment for him. He smoked and bit his thumbnail at the same time.

"I really shouldn't."

"But you want to."

"Yes."

"Then say it."

"I saw her."

"Who did you see?"

"Your friend."

"What friend?"

"The only one you have. The one who came with you on New Year's. The one who . . ."

He didn't finish the sentence.

"Did you go see her at the Institute?"

"No."

"Then . . ."

"On the outside."

"You saw her on the outside?"

"Yes."

"That can't be."

"I saw her."

"It can't be her."

"It was her."

"Where?"

"In Bell City."

He spit a piece of fingernail out and took the last puff of his cigarette before sitting down in front of Lala.

"Look, I don't think things happen by chance . . ."

"I don't care what you think. Just tell me what happened."

"My client has been after me for quite a while for us to try a threesome. She's always wanted to, but she can't talk to her husband about something like that. She's getting her revenge with me. She asked me to find her a girl and a place. It has to be far away, someone she doesn't know, and using false names. She doesn't want her maids or her friends or her children to find out.

She asked me every night if I'd found someone and I asked her to be patient, that I had a candidate in mind. . . . The truth is I had no idea what to do. The only ones I know are expensive chicks from the red-light district. And she had forbidden me from using the listings."

He lighted another cigarette.

"The owner of the Dobermans came last Wednesday. . . . You remember?"

Lala nodded.

"That guy's like you. He goes everywhere with his dogs. He brings them over here because his girlfriend lives in San Isidro, he lives in La Plata, in Bell City. . . . He was wearing his dark glasses even thought there wasn't a shred of sunlight."

Lala nodded again. Twice. She was beginning to lose her patience.

"His face looked scary. He'd been at a party the night before. In a group party. He's the kind of guy who likes to tell you every-thing, you know? But always exaggerating. When he finished, I got up my nerve and asked him if he knew any others. 'Why? Do you want me to invite you?' he said. 'Me and a client who is a woman friend . . .' 'Look, my house is way out. Better yet. And the girls aren't cheap.' 'How much?' '400.' '400?' I say to him. 'Yes, I know, a bit steep, but it's worth it. You'll see.' I asked him where his women friends were from. 'Nowhere,' he said. They bring them in and they take them away. And made it clear I wasn't to ask them any questions. I said that was fine by me. And my client would be thrilled with the anonymity. We agreed on this week-end. The guy was already putting together a get-together in his house with another couple looking for the same thing and a couple of bachelor friends. So this Saturday, when it had turned dark, we set out for Bell City.

"We were the last ones to get there. There were three single men besides the couple, the five girls, and the woman who'd brought them. They were all under twenty. The youngest wasn't even fifteen. There was a lot of alcohol, a lot of crude jokes, and a lot of laughter. The fifteen-year old was already drunk and laughed even at things that were said that were not meant to be funny. I felt sorry for her, all done up like a whore. . . . They had not come by themselves. There were two cars waiting for them outside, with two men in each car. I bet anything they were policemen. I didn't catch on right away, but later when I was in the bedroom, thinking back. . . . There's something about the sideburns, something about the clothes they wear, in the way they look at you . . . 'Okay, fellows, let's pair off,' the owner of the Doberman said. He was the first to go, grabbing a bottle of champagne and carrying off the fifteen-year-old to the bedroom."

The trainer coughed. Once, twice, three times. More out of nerves than the cigarette.

"Then I saw her. She hadn't seen me or anyone else. She had her eyes glued to the painting hanging over the fireplace. Your painting . . . ," he said as if it were the only painting in the world.

"Which one?"

"The last one you brought me."

"The Alonso?"

"He hadn't sold it, but kept it for himself."

Yikes.

I looked at Lala. If she'd listened to the story in silence up to now it was because she didn't believe it possible. The trainer had seen her once in her life and he must have been confusing her with someone else. If Guayi could leave the Institute she would not return again . . .

Lala's blood ran cold. The day of Guayi's birthday one of the guards gave her the same reply as always: she was sick and wasn't seeing visitors. Lala walked away from the Institute kicking a pebble as though it were Guayi's head. She kicked the pebble and I growled for no reason and the two of us were thinking the same thing: why was she doing that to us? We were stopped by a whistling. Lala turned around and saw her standing at one of the grated windows on the fourth floor. Guayi stuck a paper airplane, rolled as tight as a carrot, through one of the spaces of the grating. The plane glided down, turned around, glided a bit more and finally landed nose first near the pebble. Lala picked the piece of paper up and unfolded the airplane. "I saw the painting" was written on the inside. When she looked up, Guayi had disappeared.

The trainer crossed and uncrossed his arms.

"Look, I don't have any idea of what happened in your house. I don't read the papers and I don't watch TV. . . . All I know is that your friend is in prison . . . She can't be both in and out. My client realized that I was staring at your friend. . . . She asked me if I wanted her. I told her no and pointed to one of the girls sitting at the edge of the couch balancing her butt on the edge of the cushion. She was holding onto her knees to hide the way she was trembling. But you could still tell because she was twitching all over. The other couple chose your friend and the single guys chose one who had squinty eyes. That's what they wanted, to share one between them. They were more for it than the girl. The redhead . . ."

"What redhead?"

"The dame that brought them. The redhead demanded we pay her before going into the bedrooms. She counted the 1200 pesos and opened a door into an L-shaped hallway. It ran the length of the house and had three rooms, all done up as suites. Your friend and the other couple headed for the first one. They asked the redhead for the key and the redhead said the rooms had no lock but not to worry. No one was going to bother them. She put us in the room next door and continued down the hall with the single men. The room was as cloying as the rest of the house. The picture frames, the bed, the curtain rings, the rim on the furniture . . . even the knobs on the bathtub . . . all in gold. Then my client turned on the light and that's when we became upset at the age of the girl. She'd been in the shadows in the living room, with the lights down low and with candles. But seen up close with the light shining in her face . . . The mask of her makeup was just that . . ."

"How old are you?"

"Nineteen."

"Don't lie to me."

"I'm going to be nineteen in six months."

"What's your name?"

"Whatever you want."

"I get to choose?"

"You can do whatever you want."

"Then your name is Micaela . . . like mine."

"My client smiled. She'd seen this sort of thing in the movies, but the fact they were happening to her made her feel like she was sinning against . . . something . . . I don't know what. All I could do was look at the wall. I could see your friend on the other side and I couldn't stop thinking . . ."

He stopped and looked at Lala.

". . . exactly what you're thinking."

"What?"

"That she found out how to escape and is now out."

Lala replied by going over to the bed and yanked the smoothed out airplane from the wall and set it on the table. "I saw the painting," the trainer read.

"She sailed it to me from a window at the Institute," Lala said.

"Have you seen her again?"

Lala nodded.

She took the piece of paper from his hands and traced Guayi's folds. She made an airplane with the same creases.

"And afterward?" she said without looking at him.

"What?"

"What happened?"

"I couldn't stop thinking . . . about you, about her, about the guys outside. . . . That's when I said, 'They're policemen.' My client was undressing the girl and I kept rewinding the tape. When they began to undress me I said I didn't feel good. My client must have smelled on my skin the mixture of panic and revulsion because her chin began to tremble and she locked herself in the bathroom. The other Micaela sat naked on the edge of the bed. She asked me for a cigarette."

"Aren't you too young to smoke?"

"You were on the point of fucking me and you ask me that?"

"Here."

"Give me a light."

"Here. Can I ask you something . . . ?"

"No."

"It's just that . . ."

"You can't ask questions. Didn't they tell you?"

"Yes, they told me . . . But . . ."

"So, then, don't ask. Would you like me to blow you?"

The lights from an automobile lighted up the face of the trainer for a moment. He looked down and stayed that way, staring at the cement floor.

"I put my hand on her forehead to stop her. She was already kneeling on the bed. An hour later she told us our time was up. She got dressed and went to wait for us in the living room. The redhead herded them into the cars and they left."

There was a pause. That's when the trainer looked up again. He was upset, clutching his jaw, feeling the heat on his skin.

18

"I'll wait for you two hours. If you're not back by then, I'll leave."

The trainer brought the car to a stop on a dark corner, two blocks from the freeway and ten blocks from the house. There'd been a blackout and the area was like a black hole. All you could see were the lights of the cars along the streets and the candles inside some houses.

"Walk straight-ahead . . . Do you have the address?"

Lala nodded. It was written on the palm of her hand.

"Okay, off you go."

She shut the lights off and everything turned black. He didn't ask her what she intended to do. Lala put on her cotton cap, thrust her hands in her pockets and quickened her step. We found the house ten blocks down the street. It was on a corner and from what you could see from the outside it must have taken up half a block. There were three cars parked in front. We approached from the opposite sidewalk. The first car belonged to the owner of the Dobermans. There were two men dozing in the second car. A third man was reading a magazine in the last one. He looked over the cover when he saw a silhouette approaching. He turned the car lights on. The lights struck Lala in the eyes and blinded her. The man saw it was a girl, even though she walked like a man, with her back slightly bent, as if she didn't know what to do with her height. Lala stood still on the sidewalk until her eyes got used to the light. She hadn't even thought about how she'd get in the house. For a moment I thought that such an elementary detail had paralyzed her.

The man rolled down his window.

"Are you lost?"

"No."

"What's the street you want?"

"This is it."

She stopped in front of a house that was completely in the dark, rang the doorbell, and waited. The man stared at her ass.

"You're looking for someone there?"

"A boy friend."

Lala rang the doorbell again. Of course, no one answered.

"Your friend must have forgotten you were coming," the man said. "No one's home."

"He must be on his way."

She rang again.

"Can't you see there's no light on?"

He took a slug from a flask of whiskey. The cold coming in the window contaminated the stink he had generated in four hours of waiting. He leaned over to close the window on the passenger side.

"Would you give me a slug?" Lala asked.

She was already crossing over before he could say yes. She rested her elbows on the edge of the window. That's when they first saw each other's faces. "Strange," the guy thought, "when it's one of the ugly ones that turns you on." Her mouth was precious, puffed up like a biscuit. Lala raised the flask of cheap whiskey to her lips.

"That's not enough for a flea. Have some more."

He was armed and had a gun in a leather holster at his hip.

"Can I wait in there with you?"

"Sure."

Lala walked around the car. The windows of the house were lighted by candles. She could see the ones on the second floor. The ones on the first floor were hidden behind a thick hedge. The man turned the lights off when Lala got into the car. He locked the doors and turned the radio on. I was left outside, standing by the door. I could barely hear their voices, run together with the raw voice of El Cigala singing "Black Tears."

"What's your name?"

"Can you turn the heater on?"

"Are you cold?"

"A lot."

The man turned the heater on while Lala rubbed her hands together.

"Put them here."

He put her hands in front of the hot air and rubbed one of them to warm her up.

"Better?"

Lala nodded.

"Give me the other one. . . . Aren't you going to tell me your name?"

"You don't need to know."

He smiled.

"Why not."

Lala gave him her left hand while her right hand searched for his zipper. The holster with the gun was in the way. She did it suddenly, without thinking. It couldn't be all that difficult, although she had never done it before.

"I can't with that in the way," Lala said.

The man took the holster off without a moment's hesitation. He set the gun on the passenger seat. Lala wet her lips with the tip of her tongue, leaned over his legs, and opened her mouth. The car window started slowly to fog up. The man leaned back against the seat, one hand on the steering wheel and the other on Lala's head, who was already feeling for the gun on the seat, her hand on the trigger in order to slip it out. It looked deformed and ugly from her perspective. She felt something that must have been the safety catch and thought it was going to go off right then and there. It was a good ending: to die coming in a mouth like hers. But things like that don't happen in real life. He came clutching her head so she couldn't move. Lala took advantage of his ecstasy to give a final yank, taking the gun out of his holster and stuck it in her pants. She rinsed her mouth with a swig of whiskey and opened the door of the car.

"Wait . . . Don't leave," she heard the man saying to her.

But she was turning the corner of the block.

She had to disappear before the guy caught on and decided to follow her. She found a sliding gate around the corner, a garage with room for four cars. It wasn't very high. Security was guaranteed by the four Dobermans on the other side. But that was no problem for Lala and they didn't even bark. She spoke to them and stuck out her hand so they could smell her. They recognized her immediately. Lala was the one who passed out the treats at the school. They saw her climb inside the yard, wagging their tails, and jumping with joy. Once inside Lala undid the catch and slid the gate open a few centimeters to let me pass. I did the same as she did. I stood there on guard but tame, my butt stuck out so they could smell me. I didn't look them in the eye until they recognized me and stopped growling. Dobermans speak a complicated dialect, one hard to follow. But language aside, there's always the desire for everyone to be friends, so there's never any problem. We were already all friends as we crept along the perimeter of the house. Beside the blackout, there was a waning moon and the sky was blanketed. The result, seen from inside the house, was a darkness so thick that Lala could move around with ease. There was no way they could see her. The red-head was in the living room drinking a cognac in front of the fireplace. Without her guard's uniform, dressed for the night and with her hair down, it could have been difficult to recognize her. But the angry red of her head made her unmistakable. Lighted by the glow of the embers it made her look like Cruella de Vil. She'd been doing the same thing for years. She had been sent to La Plata after a murky incident at Ezeiza. Murky on the outside, because everybody on the inside knew that she was the one who beat a woman prisoner to death when she found out she was seeing someone else. The Institute was a refuge, a well-deserved vacation. She was the one who proposed this bit of business to the night-shift guards. Five girls were enough to bring in a bundle. And that's just what she needed to finish building the house on the lot she bought in Boulogne before retiring. Two of the guards were in. They brought in three friends from the force to take them and bring them and to make sure no one got out of hand. They changed the shift of the only guard who refused. He was an honorable type, but he needed the work. He forgot about the proposition and asked no more questions. Everyone had some sort of deal going on in there and no one stuck his nose in anyone else's business. The redhead checked the time. Fifteen minutes and they would have to leave.

Lala looked up. Up on the second floor the owner of the house was getting into the Jacuzzi with two of the girls. He was a criminal lawyer who had made a fortune during the ten years President Menem was in office. He never gave bottles of wine, but rather girls. He built the house in Bell City with that in mind: a gigantic love nest to party with his friends. He met the redhead in Ezeiza. It was the perfect marriage. She needed top-drawer clients and a couple of secure places and he was an old reprobate committed to his vices. Lala continued on, along the L-shaped hallway on the first floor. The three rooms were occupied. Surrounded by dogs, she stopped for a moment to contemplate the general outline of the apocalypse. Illuminated boxes filled with naked bodies kissing each other as though it was their last chance.

It was at that moment that she saw Guayi appear. She went into the bathroom of the last room, right before Lala's eyes. She turned the water on and stepped into the shower without closing the curtain. She stood there without moving. It had been months since we'd seen Guayi naked and wet like that. Lala took the gun from her waistband and put it in her pocket. On the other side of the wall, in the room, there was a couple in their fifties. When he heard the water running, the man got up from the bed and walked toward the bathroom.

"Don't take a shower. . . . We're not done yet."

"I'll be right back," Guayi said, rubbing her body.

She was about to get out when she suddenly looked out the window. All she could see was her own blurred and faint reflection on the barely steamed up window. Lala didn't move. They were separated by a pane of glass, so close to each other that Guayi steamed it up even more with her breath. She could hear the patter of the dogs as she wiped the glass with the palm of her hand. No sooner had she left the bathroom than Lala's hands pushed the window all the way open. She sat on the frame. She was neither afraid nor nervous. The anguish of the last year had disappeared. She felt instead such an angry lucidity that even the air made her woozy. The door of the bathroom was open and if she could see the bed, they could only see her by looking up.

"You're going to have to take another bath."

"So what?"

"You're all pale."

"Do you feel okay?"

"A little dizzy."

"Come here. Put your head down."

"No, really, I feel all right now. . . . What do you want to do?"

"Before anything else I want you to feel okay . . . ," the woman insisted, feeling as though her maternal instinct had been awakened even in the most unusual circumstances.

"We paid $400 for her . . . So she can put up with the dizziness a little bit, okay?"

"Don't behave like an animal, Patricio."

"I'm fine, really. Don't fight . . . We can do whatever you want."

Seen from outside, Guayi was a stroke of harmony in the middle of a grotesque jumble of arms and legs. It must even have made an impact on the Dobermans. They left me alone on the other side of the window, holding my breath until the woman looked up and screamed. Lala was standing at the foot of the bed. The woman hunched up in a corner. The man grabbed for his underpants. Guayi was left in the middle of the bed, looking at Lala as if the Virgin had appeared.

"What are you doing here?"

"Get dressed."

The man looked from one to the other.

"Do you know each other? Do you know her?"

"Shut up," Lala told him. "Let go of that."

The man continued to get dressed. Lala took out the gun she had in her pocket and pointed it at him.

"I told you to let go of that."

This time he paid attention to her.

"Don't hurt us, please. Don't hurt me . . ."

"Tell him to shut up."

But the woman continued to sob.

"Gag her with this."

She pointed to the underwear with the gun.

"Please . . ."

"Do what I say."

The man grabbed his underwear, wound it like a blindfold, and sat down in front of the woman.

"Open your mouth."

"No."

"Sweetheart, please."

The women opened her mouth and the man gagged her with his underpants. The silence was a relief for Lala. Her hands were shaking and her orders sounded false. She was making it up as she went along. But she was making it up holding a loaded gun. The man realized she was more afraid than he was. Rather than calming him down, Lala's fear made him freeze.

"Tie his hands together."

Using her bra the woman tied her husband's hands to the headboard of the bed.

"What are you going to do with us?"

"Not a thing. If you keep quiet, nothing will happen to you."

She turned to Guayi.

"Get dressed."

"How did you find out . . . ?"

". . . that you were here? By chance. Get dressed."

Guayi's black dress lay on the floor. She put the man's jeans on, his sweater, and his jacket. Lala watched her get dressed.

"There're three armed guards at the door."

"Two."

She showed her the gun.

"If you don't help me, I'm going to take you out by force. As a hostage," Lala said to Guayi.

"What kind of hostage? They'll get us both."

"We'll use them as a shield," Lala said, pointing her gun at the couple.

Guayi smiled. It was things like this that made her love her so much. Lala lived in a made-up world of action movies, stories in the newspaper, battles, princes, and dragons.

But in the end she was capable of murder.

The woman forgot about her husband when she thought about being used as a shield and took advantage of a moment of distraction to run toward the door. She managed to open it before Guayi grabbed her by the hair. The man thought Lala was going to shoot.

He screamed.

The hallway filled with the sound of feet.

The redhead opened the door. She saw the man tied to the bed . . . the woman silenced by a gag . . . and Guayi dressed like a man. She grabbed for her gun and we heard a shot. Lala had aimed for her head, but hit the arm instead. The redhead slid down the wall and the rug around her turned red. She tried to get her gun, but Guayi already had it. Lala kicked the door shut. She opened the window and saw the policemen running toward the house.

The window shattered. We dove for the floor.

Guayi thought Lala had gone mad when she heard her whistle. Then she saw the Dobermans come running from the shadows. She thought they were black angels when she saw them take wing in response to the cry of Attack! Our teeth tore at necks and arms and legs with the fury of a pack of wolves. The guns went off three or four times more, but skyward and the buzzing sound didn't come from the bullets but the cries. Only one of them managed to shake me off. He fired. My body didn't react when I tried to move. He killed one of the other dogs before Lala did the same to him.

And, then, suddenly silence.

The panting of the Dobermans blended with Lala's. The trainer always said those dogs could destroy the body of a man in five minutes. He said five as though reading from a manual. That night we found out it was true. I felt the ground under me. Lala picked me up in her arms.

"You'll be fine."

The shot fired by the owner of the house came from the second floor. Lala fell to her knees but didn't let go of me. He got her in the right leg. He didn't know how to shoot either. He had bought the gun together with the house, the clothes, and the dogs. The man felt the gunshot as though he were coming. Excited, he took aim again, but didn't manage to shoot because one of the girls took advantage of the uproar and knocked him over.

Guayi grabbed the redhead by her hair and tied her hands with her belt.

"You're coming with us."

"You won't make it."

She exited the room shoving her forward. She helped Lala get up. She carried me in her arms. She saw her friends standing in the windows. Two in the downstairs rooms and two on the terrace. They weren't going to try to escape. They were going to wait for the police to take them back to the Institute. The scandal was going to make them stars for a few weeks. Two or three at the most. Then they would be forgotten in one of the women's prisons. They went out the front door. The neighbors closed their doors and windows. The sirens were getting closer and closer. The cars stood open, one of them with the keys in it.

Guayi laid me on the passenger seat.

She got into the back seat with the redhead.

Lala took the wheel.

They were halfway to the trainer's place.

Guayi opened the door and shoved the redhead from the car. Lala yanked the steering wheel.

The car appeared at the end of the block. Rather, we appeared, because the trainer's Taunus was parked in the same spot with the lights off. Lala continued to hold my wound shut, yelling at me not to close my eyes. But my body was fading. The trainer didn't ask any questions, not even when he saw us covered with blood. He used his sweater to stop the hemorrhaging and picked Lala up in his arms and carried her over to the car.

"Open the trunk."

He placed Lala inside.

"You, too."

Guayi lay down beside Lala. She put an arm under her head and hugged her against her body. The trainer patted my head before he set me on top of them. The echo of the hood of the trunk lasted a good while. The Taunus started to move.

Our bodies were so jumbled together that we didn't know where one left off and the other began. Lala's feverish delirium began to confuse even Guayi, who tried to stay calm, breathing through the slit that allowed her to see that the trainer had not taken the freeway but was going along a dark dangerous dirt street.

"I saw your son . . ."

"What?"

"The fish boy."

I felt something warm on my skin. It was Lala's blood. The sweater was not enough to stop the flow. Guayi moved me out of the way, felt in the dark for the wound and applied pressure.

"We swam together in the lake. I painted him on the walls of the house . . ."

"Shh . . ."

"Your grandfather told me the whole story."

"That's enough, Lala."

"You don't have to lie to me."

"I'm not lying."

"Then, tell me."

"What?"

"Anything."

"The old man made up a story because he can't handle what I did."

Guayi's voice was stuck in her throat. It was no longer the deep voice that made people look at her twice, as if they could not fathom such a heavy voice in such a slight body. Now it was a hoarse whisper, a confession she murmured in Lala's ear, broken sentences, fractured by her tears as if guilt had been there all along.

". . . He was so weak, so small, he wasn't even strong enough to cry, and he grew worse and worse each day. . . . I saw myself

alone in that house, without my grandfather, alone with him. . . .
'I'm doing it for him,' is what I thought . . . I was doing it for him,
so he could sleep soundly, so he could rest. . . . It was easier that
way, holding his head for a minute, just one minute, underwater,
it was easier . . ."

She spit the words out as she held Lala's body, cradling her as
she had done in that other place as dense and dark as this one.
And suddenly her arms ceased to hold her, opening to let her go,
and Lala felt herself sinking to the bottom. I saw the eyes of both
of them in the dark, giant-sized, popping out, trying to understand that glass of poisoned milk and that embrace in the depths
of the lake that had transformed them, in a blink of an eye, into
what they were.

"The cold remained inside me . . . The cold of the water . . . I
can't get rid of it . . . I can't. Not even when I met you."

That's what Guayi said, but it could have been Lala.

"Until the day I saw you stirring that glass of milk . . . I asked
you what you were doing. . . . Do you remember what you said to
me?"

Of course she remembered. I also remembered.

"'I'm doing it for him. I'm doing him a favor,' is what you said.
The same lie, the same eyes. Your hands even trembled like
mine. I stood watching you climb the stairs and that's when all of
a sudden I understood. I didn't do it for him. I did it for me."

She repeated it twice, like a sentence.

"For me."

She didn't say another word, but her body was colder than
ever. Lala held her by the waist and closed her eyes. Guayi

placed one hand on her head and the other on mine. They remained silent, breathing the air that was left, devoid of tears and secrets, while the Taunus picked up speed and the road smoothed out.

The trainer brought the car to a stop on a deserted block near Constitution Station. He opened the door and found us lying still, flattened, one having settled into the spaces left by the other, our eyes squinting from the glow from a streetlight. He smiled at me before picking me up in his arms, surprised I was still there.

"Climb out."

He banged on a metal safety door until an upstairs light came on. A bald guy stuck his head out the window and muttered a curse he cut short the minute he recognized the trainer. A few minutes later he opened a side door to let us in. We followed him single file down a narrow corridor. I guessed it before he turned the light on, because the aroma was something divine. The first thing I saw was a bag of balanced diet, bagged cow dung no matter how you looked at it, but caviar for a starving dog. There were three Sheepdog puppies sleeping on top of each other in the window, a fish tank, two rabbits fucking in a cage, food, toys. . . . Every time I blinked the landscape changed, the hall to the veterinarian's office, from the office to the operating room. . . . The only thing that didn't change, holding me, were the arms of the trainer and Lala's eyes, begging me not to let go. The bald guy, who besides being a veterinarian, was the trainer's older brother, led the way to the back and turned the light on. A cat meowed from one of the metal stretchers. His back was shaved and he had a scar that ran from one end to the other. He laid it on the desk and handed the bag of serum to Guayi.

"Hold it."

He lay Lala down on the same stretcher. He cut her pants leg so he could inspect the wound.

"What did you get messed up in?" he asked the trainer.

"I need you to stop the blood. That's all."

The veterinarian's wife appeared in the doorway in a night gown and slippers. It wasn't the first time her brother-in-law had showed up in the middle of the night with a wounded animal. But this was different. She wasn't going to risk everything for two strangers.

"I want you to leave."

"They'll be gone in half an hour. You take care of the dog and I'll take care of the girl."

They worked in silence for fifteen minutes, each one at his stretcher, using Guayi and the trainer as nurses. Lala never shut her eyes for a moment and kept looking at me. She was luckier than I was. Her bullet had nicked her femur and exited. Mine struck a vein. When they were done, the bald guy pointed to a hose in the back patio for Guayi to wash the blood away. His wife brought a pair of pants from upstairs, gave the trainer some painkillers and asked them to leave. They weren't the only one to send us on our way without questions. The trainer stopped in front of the station.

"You're on your own from here on out."

The trainer took the cage out of the car and emptied his wallet in Lala's hands. Her final salary, in advance. Enough to get them out of the country. He stood watching them disappear, Guayi dragging me in my cage with one hand and Lala by the waist with the other to hide her limp.

The cage wasn't necessary. The five o'clock bus wasn't a regular one and it had no luggage compartment. The bags traveled on the roof and the animals on the inside. Anyone who didn't like it could wait for the eight o'clock departure. Guayi made Lala comfortable on one of the seats in back, left the cage by the side of the bus and carried me in her arms. Kneeling on the floor and petting me, she made my body comfortable next to Lala's feet. Before she let go, I licked her hand one last time, a wet kiss on her open palm. When she withdrew her hand it had blood on it, no more than a drop. Lala rubbed me all over with her naked foot, not looking at me, with her head resting against the back of the seat and her eyes closed.

"All right?"

Guayi didn't answer. She opened my mouth, ran the tip of a finger over my tongue and withdrew it again stained with blood. Now it was a heavier drop, darker. She lowered her head so it rested on my snout. She stayed there, snuggled up to me, wordless, without moving. Her tears were as sweet as the water in the lake.

"Go to sleep," she said whispering in my ear after a while. "Now I'm taking care of her."

When she stood up she had my blood on her forehead, her

mouth, all over. Lala didn't see it. She wiped herself with the sleeve of her sweatshirt before sitting down beside her.

"He's going to be okay."

She said it as she watched Lala's foot caressing me, the bus pulling out of the terminal. If she moved it just a little bit, she would rest it in a pool of blood. Guayi broke open the ampoule of painkiller with her teeth and hurriedly prepared the syringe, as though she were the one in pain. She did everything with the thought that they were going to come for them at any moment. Guayi brushed her hair away from her face and rested her lips on Lala's, while with her other hand she lowered Lala's pants a few centimeters so the syringe could penetrate her skin.

"Like that . . . ," Lala said, feeling Guayi's breath more than the shot. "Kiss me now and it's all over."

"What's all over?"

Lala didn't answer, but kept on petting me in silence. She didn't know what, but something was all over.

"This is a happy ending . . ."

"I don't know," Guayi said.

"Yes . . ."

"I guess it is."

Happy endings made her feel bad and left her saying over and over the same thing.

". . . And then what?"

"I don't know."

"Make something up."

"I don't know."

Only when the bus left Buenos Aires behind did they look each other in the eyes. They were sitting there but they were still running. Guayi lifted her tee-shirt and injected herself with remaining third of the painkiller, down to the last drop. They stayed that way, not taking their eyes off each other, while their anguish faded.

"We have the house," Lala said.

"Yes."

"And the lake."

"Yes . . ."

"Will you go swimming with me?"

"To the very depths," Guayi said.

It was the last thing I heard before sinking into sleep. By the time the bus got to the country no one was awake. There's nothing harder than resisting group slumber. Even Guayi gave in. As the bus drew near the border, the air filled with the echo of other people's dreams, a stew in which, in the end, we all dream the same thing.